Rants and Raves

by
Nathan Leslie

PublishAmerica
Baltimore

© 2002 by Nathan Leslie.

All rights reserved. No part of this book may be reproduced in any form without written permission from the publishers, except by a reviewer who may quote brief passages in a review to be printed in a newspaper or magazine.

First printing

ISBN: 1-59129-856-3
PUBLISHED BY PUBLISHAMERICA BOOK PUBLISHERS
www.publishamerica.com
Baltimore

Printed in the United States of America

This book is dedicated to Julie, whose love and support provides the constant counter-balance to the dark matter I portray here.

Acknowledgements

I'd like to especially thank Matt Katz and Lawrence-Minh Davis, who both went out of their way to offer critical assistance and encouragement to this collection, Cindy Schaeffer, who offered many helpful tips, and Reg McKnight, who helped unleash the monsters from their lairs. Stories from this collection have been published in the following journals: "The Lock" in *Wascana Review*, "The Ring" in *Adirondack Review*, "Escort" in *Branches*, "Man to Man" in *Unlikely Stories*, "July Burn" in *The Brooklyn Rail*, "The Mending" in *Nasty*, "The Pillar Ascetic" in *Pig Iron Malt*, "The Abject" in The Moonwort Review, and "The Phrenologist" in *3rd Warrior Review*.

Table Of Contents

The Mending	9
The Lock	20
Dross	30
The Ballad of Ted and Maddie	43
Eggs	53
The Abject	65
Escort	78
Toothpick Jones and the Hounds' Tongue Cave	89
The Ring	97
Slut	104
The Phrenologist	109
The Pillar Ascetic	120
July Burn	125
Retreat	134
Works-in-Progress	140
Man to Man	151
The Rationalist	164
Cows	178

THE MENDING

If I bend close enough, I can almost hear the buzzing. He's leaning over me like he always does. I can smell his wallet smell and the stuff he puts on his neck. It smells like dog hair. There's steak and green beans on his breath. There's a ketchup smell, and onions. Usually I can feel him standing over me while I sleep. It doesn't make me feel weird or anything. It's what he likes to do. I love him. If he's standing there, most of the time I just ignore him. This time it's hot, and I sit up. He asks me to lean closer to hear the buzzing. I lean close, but I can't hear it. I tell him I can, because maybe I can't hear it like adults can. Maybe I just don't know how to hear right. I don't want to make him upset.

"Son, we're going on a little venture," he says to me. "A little trip." I am very sleepy. My eyes feel burny and tired. It's hot. I smell my own sweat. I want to swim. I can hear the fan turning in the window. The clock says 11:30. I usually go to sleep at 9:00. I nod and nod and nod, and then feel his arm hair against my face, and me lifting in the air, and then I hear metal jingling and the walking sounds, and I also hear more metal against metal, and then the door shuts. I can feel his muscles harden under me and twist around. He's a strong man. He says I will be like him someday. I don't know how I'll ever be as strong as him though. I hear the car door opening. He places me softly on the back seat. Things are happening so slow, like I'm dreaming and living at the same time. I smell rope and other stuff in the back seat, and pine needles, and then his car door opens. Now it smells like all kinds of things from the outside. Flowers, and bark, and trees I don't know. Leaves from the trees. Stems from the leaves. Dirt and whatever is beneath the dirt. It makes me feel sleepy.

"This is just something we have to do," he says. I nod again. He starts the car, and we whirrrrrrrrrrrrrrrrrr backwards, and then stop, and then go forward. I like the sound a car makes going backward.

It sounds like it runs on batteries then, but it doesn't. It is a good sound, and I feel safe in the back seat. I'm not wearing a seat belt, but I don't have to since I'm laying down. I can't hear the crickets or the fan. I can hear a man talking low and deep from the back and sides. Then another man talking, then some music. "I can turn the radio down," my father says. The talking gets quieter. I'm half-asleep. I can hear the whoosh of the air conditioning, and I can smell that clean air-conditioning smell. It's like the refrigerator. Do all machines smell this way? I want to ask him, but instead I fall asleep. It feels like a long time.

Then we're stopped. I lift my head and all I can see is darkness, and then nothing. Darkness and trees in the darkness. The clock says 3:30. The lights switch off, and the car door opens and closes. I am there, just waiting to see what happens. I rub my face, and I rub my eyes. I can hear my father's boots in the gravel: chhh, chhhh, chhhh, chhh, chhh, chhh. Then the back door swings open, and he lifts me out of the backseat, and onto his back. This is how he carries me usually. It's better for my back that way. My back is curved, and I need to get a rod in it. The doctors told me that it's pretty normal. Many boys have curved backs. I haven't met any, but when I do, we'll compare. Mine looks like the letter R. Not the straight part. Maybe another boy has a J or a P. I'm not scared about the rod. I'm not scared of doctors. Maybe it'll be a good thing to happen.

My father and I can talk about not being perfect a lot, because he's got that thing where you hear sounds all the time in your ear. If I get an operation, my dad can rest with me in the hospital, and maybe we can share a room. My dad rests a lot. He listens to music a lot, and leaves the television on, and tries to talk. He says he doesn't want to hear himself. He hears a buzzing, but sometimes he says it sounds more like a crackling. Like a fire in his ears. He says he got it from my mother. He says it was something he didn't know could happen until it happened. He says he can't stop thinking about it. He says all he hears is bzzzzzzzzzzzzzzzz. Bzzzzzzzzzzzzzzz. Bzzzzzzzzzzzzzzz. Sometimes, he says he tapes a pillow over his head with that gray kind of tape to stop the buzzing. But it doesn't stop the buzzing though, he says. It just makes it buzz more in the pillow and less in his head. When he sleeps, he always has a radio on, or the television.

Then my father lifts me, and I can smell the woods all around. I know the smell of honeysuckle, and I ask him if I can eat some. He shakes his head without saying anything. My father never says no. He says yes. He says my mother says no a lot. I don't hear it. My father seems serious tonight, and not talkative. Usually my father tries not to be serious. My father usually talks all the time so he doesn't have to listen to the buzz or the crackle. He scratches my hair with his fingers. I can feel his arm hair against my cheeks. If I listen closely, I can hear the arm hair against me.

"Just try not to worry," he says. "Be brave."

"I won't worry," I say. Then my father ties a rope around my back, and around his waist, and I can hear the rope brush against the other parts of the rope when he pulls it tight. It feels tight but good to be against his back. I can see other parked cars around on white gravel. It's so white it glows. Nobody's in the cars. My father holds my knees up for support and walks right into the woods. I can hear his steps in the leaves. It's darker than my room at night. My father doesn't have a flashlight, and I wonder why. Questions come to me. How does he see? Has he been here before? I am surprised my father isn't talking to me, but he's busy. Maybe the woods will be like the radio. I guess I get quiet if I'm busy too. It takes silence to concentrate. Why? And why do we need to concentrate? I want to ask him. But I don't want to bother him.

My father pats my knee as we go, like he's playing a drum sound. I can smell sap and pine needles now, and my father whispers to me that we only have to go a mile or so like this. It's not hard for my father to carry me. I wonder if his red hair helps him be strong. Fireflies blink on and off. Blink. Unblink. Then we go down a hill, and my father trips on something. Pain jolts through my back, and the rope burns my skin. My head is shaken. More pain. Then he catches himself on a tree, and he says sorry. My back hurts.

We start off again. My eyes are starting to see in the dark, but it's just woods everywhere. Everything is a blur. My father's footsteps are light on the leaves and dirt. My back hurts with each step he takes, but it's just normal hurt. The rod will help the hurt. The operation will help even more. But then, after the operation, I won't be as special. My father clears his throat. I lean close so maybe I can hear what he hears, but I still can't. I can hear every step crunch and lift. Crunch and uncrunch. A tree branch whips me on the arm and face, and I cry out. He is going so fast. Crunch. Uncrunch. Crunch. Uncrunch.

"Son," he says.

"Yes," I say. I'm holding on to his neck, and I can feel the sweat start to wet it. I can smell some of the sweat on his shoulders. His shirt feels damp.

"You know I have this thing called tinnitus, right. I've told you that," he says. There are so many fireflies now. Blink. Unblink. Blink. Unblink. They make connect-the-dot patterns in the trees. I can see the trees in the blinks.

"Yes," I say.

"Well, that's the main reason we're here now tonight. I couldn't leave you all alone at the house, so here we are. And there are other reasons. But this lady we're going to see can only meet me late at night. Understand?"

"Yes," I say. We're walking along a creek now. I can hear the gurgle, gurgle, gurgle. I can hear the water over the rocks, and in the clearer places. I can smell a fire burning in the distance. I can see smoke. Or I think I can. Maybe it's just the darkness or clouds, but it looks like smoke. I can hear somebody yelling. Ohhhhhhhhhhhhhh. Oooooooooooooo. It sounds deep, like they are in water, or in a cave. I don't feel hot anymore. Fireflies blink.

"Son," he says. "Some jobs are dangerous, and that's how I got this ringing thing. I wasn't always a cook. I've never told you how I got it. I got it when I used to work for a place where they have concerts and things. This is way back."

"Oh," I say. I feel better now that he's telling me. It was always just a mystery to me. I like mysteries, but sometimes it's too much. I feel good for a moment. I can almost enjoy going along. Crunch. Uncrunch. Crunch. "I thought it just happened."

"Sort of. It did just happen," he says. "It happened because your mother got me this job at this place. They played music, which was part of my job to manage, and I never thought anything would happen out of that. But it did. It did. The music gave me this buzzing. That's why I usually don't listen to much music anymore. You never know what will be dangerous, see."

"Oh," I say. We cross over a short bridge, and more gurgling water. I can smell more plants and mud, and I think moss. Blink. Unblink. Blink. There are rocks in the blinks.

"Music is very dangerous sometimes. And I, um, I guess I'm angry at your mother for this," he says. "Her idea. But there's more to it than that, you know. That's probably the way to put it. If you want to put it that way. The reason is that I don't think that had to happen. When, she uh, got pregnant with you, we both had to leave college, and I could never really go back. Her parents sent her back. Made her go back. That's why I had to work. My work was that music situation, son. I've never told you any of this."

"No," I say. The fire is stronger. The yelling is louder. I don't see as many fireflies. Ohhhhhhhhhhhhhhhhhhhh. Ooooooooooooooo. Ohhhhhhhhhhhhhhhhh. Crunch. Uncrunch.

"I don't want you to think less of me. So I'm not mad at you. It's not your fault, son. It's not your mother's fault either. It's just what happened, but you see it could have been…different," he says. Then suddenly I feel a pain in my back, pain in my back, pain in my back. Buzzzzzzzzz. I straighten. Better. Blink. Unblink. Ohhhhhhh.

"So she's gone now, and I know you miss her, and I miss her too, but I'm trying to help myself. That's why we're walking through the woods at this hour. This woman is going to help me. The doctors can't help me, even if they could I can't afford them right now. You know those men I see sometimes? The ones from Wednesdays and Fridays?"

"Yes," I say. I can hear drumming, and some metal hitting metal in the distance. The smoke smell is stronger. It seems like we're going down, and then up, and then he steps over something.

"Those men try to help me. They make me feel better about myself, inside and outside. See. That way I can make stained glass. That way I can go to work. I have my needs. I also have my pleasures. Sometimes the needs and pleasures go together, if that makes sense." This is the way my father talks when he tries to block out the buzzing, cause I can't understand him at all. He just talks to shut out the buzzzzzzzzzzzzzzzzzzzzzzzzz. I can never understand him. "This is why I send you to an all boys school," he says. "Girls become women, and women become women like your mother. They want lots of things, and they want you to do all the work. And there's nothing in the world you can do to disagree. You disagree, and you are left in the dust. And you can't battle a woman. You don't have the tools. With a boy, you can punch him in the face. That's clear. It's honest. It's simple. But with girls...it's different. There is nothing plain about it."

I decide to just listen and try to understand, because I'm getting lost. And the sounds are becoming louder and louder. I think of Gary and Henry, and how they brought me gifts. They would give me beer to try through a loopy straw, and played War with me and Go Fish. They'd let me bet with potato chips. They drove me to school if my father was busy.

"Have you ever kissed a girl, son?"

"No," I say. The drumming and clanking is getting louder and louder. No more blinking.

"That's good then. I don't mind. Women are the enemy in some ways. They are the natural enemy that men have. That's why we sort of hunt them down. It's built into who we are from the beginning, and anything you try to do to alter it isn't going to happen. Understand? That's why we don't treat them right. It's okay to do something different..." His voice fades off, and he coughs. "I don't want to tell you what to do or not to do," he says. "I just want to warn you how the world is, okay?"

"Oh," I say. I can smell the fire burning stronger. Crunch. Uncrunch. Crunch.

"This woman we're going to see, she's going to help me with my ears. Or try to at least. I don't want you to grow up hating people, son. I don't hate anybody, except women are, you know... But I guess I can't help that with everything that happened. This is my big chance to heal myself of that too. If she can help me, I know that will help with my feelings too."

The more we walk, the louder the drumming becomes. Then we come out of the woods into a lighter open area. It's a sort of field with a house made of boards in the middle of it. There is a group of men sitting in the weeds in front of the porch. Some of the men play drums, and some are hitting metal together, like pipes and pans, and those flat things you see next to drums. Short little statues sit on the porch. They all play together and don't look at me or my father. Some of the men wear hats over their faces as they bang the pipes and pans. I wonder why, but I don't ask. Some of the men whoop at certain times. I can hear somebody moaning or yelling inside the house. Ohhhhhhhhhhhhhh.

My father unties me, and I stand behind him. It hurts to stand. He piles the rope next to him, and we sit in the group. That feels better. There must be ten or twelve men. My father and I are the only people not hitting something or playing something. A man from the back hands my father two pipes. My father hands me one. My father and I hit our pipes together, over and over and over. I don't know why. We just do it. Clank, clank, clank.

The man we're sitting next to has short curly hair and deep brown eyes. He looks at me like he wants to ask a question. Maybe he's wondering what I'm doing there. He smells like smoke and sweat. He leans over to my father.

"She has the touch," he says. Clank, clank, clank.

"Right," my father says. "That's why I'm here." Clank. Clank. Clank. There are small statues on the porch. There is a pounding in the house. On one side there is a window. It's open, but I can't see anything. The door is open too, but I can only see how it opens into the dark. My father looks curious. He asks the man next to us if we can sit on the porch, and the man shakes his head. Ohhhhhhhhhhhhh. Oooooooooooooo.

"Each healing must be separate," he says. "It's a taboo to know what each one is about, understand? So she has us play the drums for that." My father nods like he knows what's going on and wants the man to stop talking. Looking down at the dirt, I see that the man's left leg is crooked. I wonder if he walks crooked. The drumming and clanking keep going and going.

"You've been before," my father says. Clank, clank.

"Twice. It helped me."

"Do other people seem healed too?"

"It looks that way," the man says. "Just think about those statues. You know what they are, right?" Ooooooooooooooooooo.

"No," my father says.

"I can't remember what they're called either. But it was big way back when. I mean before anything. It was real important back then."

They keep talking, but after hours of drumming, I fall asleep. I don't understand. I want to ask lots of whys. I lean against my father. I don't remember seeing men come or go, but when I sit up, my father is the only one still clanking. Clank. All the other men are gone. The sky is getting lighter. I can't see the stars anymore, just the moon. The fire is dead, but I can still smell smoke. There is more moaning coming from inside the house. It lasts forever. Ohhhhhhhhhhhhhhhhhhhhhhhh. Ooooooooooooooooooooo.

Finally the man comes out, covered in a robe. I can't see his face, and he runs directly into the woods. I can see his shape move through the trees, and up the hill to where the cars are. Then I look into the darkness of the house. The woman shuffles in the darkness, and steps onto the porch. She's a huge woman. She has a black robe on with thin red flower designs snaking all over it. The thin part of the flower is yellow and white. The stem is invisible. Her fat is hanging out of the robe. Her face is covered with red marks. There are places where fat drops from her face. Her fingers are short and fat like little sausages.

"Last one," she says to the air. She turns to go inside, and my father takes my hand, and we follow her. It's hard for me to walk. My back is on fire. I can feel rub burns from the rope. We walk onto the porch, and the woman turns slowly. She hears and sees me. She seems like she knows a lot. I wonder if she really does. I wonder how old she is.

"What is this? One person only," she says. "What is this?" My father tries to tell her that he can't leave me outside all by myself. He asks her if I can't come in. She asks my father how old I am, and he tells her. She says it's okay this time. I'm too young, she says. But it doesn't matter. Last customer. "I'm too tired to care," she says. She smells sweet and sweaty. She smells like the stuff my father puts on his neck. The smell is everywhere though. It might be a candle, or something else. There is black dirt beneath her fingernails. Her hair glows in the light. It looks red, but when I blink, it's brown.

The inside of the house is one big room. There is nothing in the room but two chairs and a table with a candle, and a thin stick with smoke coming from it, and a jar of water on it. The candle crackles. I wonder if that's what the buzzing sounds like. Maybe it doesn't sound like that. Next to the chairs and the table is a low bed. The bed is big. There is a stack of sheets and towels next to the bed. I don't see any food. I wonder how she got so fat. I sit in the corner by the door. My back still hurts. It is dark. The woman takes my father's hand, and tells him to put his donation on the table under the jar of water. He reaches into his pocket and looks back at me. His eyes look sad. It looks like he's going to throw up, and I wonder if he needs to go to the bathroom. I don't understand. She tells him to lie down on his back. Then he looks away from me. He doesn't throw up or anything. He just looks sad in his eyes. His body is loose.

"Close your eyes now," she says. "I'm going to take care of you." Crackle. Crackle.

The woman holds her hands over the candle for a moment, then rubs them together slowly over the flame. I wonder if it kills the germs too. Crackle. Crackle. She kneels above my father, and picks his shirt up with two fingers. She slides her hands under his shirt. Suddenly she slaps her hands on my father's chest, and I can hear the flesh on flesh.

"I heal with love," she says. "My touch sends love to you. Feel it? Concentrated love. What is your affliction?"

"I have tinnitus," my father says. He starts telling her about the doctors. The candle starts hissing too. Hissssssss.

"What is it?"

"My ears ring or buzz all the time. I just want it to stop. It's driving me crazy. I can't sleep. I can't take care of my son. I can't do anything the right way."

I watch the woman rubbing my father's back, and then she takes his pants off. She rubs my father's legs with her hands. Then his hair and head. Hisssssssssssssssss.

"Everything will be just fine," she says. "Everything is going to be okay." She rubs his arms and hands. Then she takes her robe off, and lies on my father's back. My father grunts. It must be heavy. The woman lifts herself with her arms, and turns my father around. Then she kisses my father all over, and puts his wee-wee all over her, in her mouth over and over again. Ohhhhhhhhhhhh. Oooooooooooo. I close my eyes then open them again. I don't want to see, but I see. Then the woman jumps up and down on my father over and over, and this is when I hear my father moan like the others. It must hurt with all the fat, and she smells funny. Like sweat but stronger. I wonder if it's healing the buzzing, and if it could heal my back.

"Some men say no," the woman says when she's jumping. "You never said no."

"I just figured," my father says. Ooooooooooooo. Ohhhhhhhhhhhh.

"It is part of the healing," she says. Hisssssssssssssssssssssss.

"I hope so," my father says.

"You will have to come back to be healed all the way," she says. She's almost out of breath.

"Okay," my father says. "You're like some kind of earth goddess, aren't you? You're like the kind that existed...that people are talking about." He's talking like he does when he has beers. His voice sounds heavy. Her voice sounds lighter. Ooooooooooooooo.

"If you say so," the woman says. "Do you feel better?"

"I think so," my father says. "How couldn't I?" Hissssssssssssss. Ohhhhhhhhhh.

Then the moaning and shouting gets louder, and it starts to smell even worse from the sweat. Then it smells like other things I've never smelled before. That's when I start thinking about other things. I don't know why. I close my eyes and try to think about riding my bike down a street with lots of trees and flowers in the sun. The whole house seems to be shaking from the woman's jumping up and down. Then a statue falls from the porch into the dirt. Ooooooooooooo. Ohhhhhhhhhhhhhh. I turn around to look, and I see another one fall. It shakes with each jump, jump, jump. The window rattles. I hide my eyes in my arm and knee. I smell the grass stains on my knees. I don't remember how they got there. I feel the rough skin of my knee with my cheek. Then it stops. I lift my head and I watch another one of the clay statues fall headfirst onto the top step of the porch. It lands with a thud. It doesn't break, but it rolls over and over again onto the front. When I look at the front of the statue, I can see it is a statue of a woman like her. It is fat and round with a fat round head, and big lumps everywhere. All the statues are the same.

Then everything slows down and the jumping stops, and the sky is lighter from the sun. I can feel the heat coming from outside. The woman walks over and drinks from the jar. She asks my father if he wants some. She asks me if I want some. I shake my head, but she says come on over and drink from the jar. My father stares at me with his sad eyes. I get up slowly and walk. It is hard for me to walk straight. I can't do the balance beam at school or anything. I kind of hop over there.

I take the jar and imagine all the other people that have touched it, and drank from it. My teacher would say I shouldn't drink from it because of the germs, and so would my mother, and so would my grandmother in Seattle. The outside of the jar smells like sweat, and the lines in the glass are fuzzy with dirt. The jar is wet with water that drips down it. I'm thirsty. I press my mouth to the jar and take a sip. The water is warm and salty-tasting, and I spit it at my feet. My father doesn't say anything. She doesn't say anything. "Take one of those statues with you," the lady finally says.

I look at my father. His head is turned in a funny angle, and he's wearing a robe, just like the man who ran into the woods. His chin is against his chest, like he is in trouble or something, and his hair is sweaty. I expect him to look better, but his eyes look worse. The lines on his forehead are out, and his mouth is small. He puts his hand over his ear, and presses his head further down into the pillow. He sighs. Then he sighs again. I don't understand why, but I take another sip of the water. I try to swallow, but I spit it out again, and the woman takes the jar from my hands. Her eyes are on fire.

My father says he's ready to go. He holds one hand over his ear and walks by me quickly. It is almost light out. I can see the sun glow behind the trees, and the birds are chirping. He doesn't look at me, and he doesn't pick me up. He walks quickly into the woods, right back the way we came. I follow after him the best I can. I pick up one of the statues. I hold it for balance, and I hop after him.

THE LOCK

Before Alec leaves his house, he must wash his hands. Alec must curl and uncurl his hands six times in a fresh white cotton towel that has been washed twice and dried twice, and bleached many times, but never hung out to dry. Then he must shower for ten and a half minutes in cold water, and wash himself three times with oatmeal soap and three types of shampoo, and dry himself on another fresh white towel that has never been used before. Then he must repeat the steps. After he has dried himself again, he must dress himself in brand new clothes that have never been used before, by himself or anyone else, and he must brush the oak cross twice over each fiber of the clothes, and over any exposed skin. He must protect himself from contamination.

Alec brushes the cross over the receiver before he allows it near his ear, and he calls Cara. He issues forth a prayer as he listens to the phone ring: "Dear Lord, please do not allow them to infiltrate this body, which is pure, and which is part of You and Your creation. Lord, please do not allow them to spoil Your handiwork."

"Hi, Cara?"

"Hi Alec," she answers. "I'm glad you called. I was wondering–"

"Me too," he says. He holds the phone next to his ear without allowing the plastic to touch his ear. Through his slacks he can feel the cool scissor blades in his pocket. He can feel the jewelry box in his other pocket.

"What would you like to do tonight?" Cara sounds as if she anticipated his call, as if she was biding her time until he called. Alec isn't sure how he feels about this. Of course there will be no hand-holding, much less kissing. They will eat at a quiet restaurant, carefully though, quietly, chewing quietly so they can't hear each other's chewing. They will listen to soft music while they eat, and after they eat they can take a walk as long as they just look around and talk – but not too much, and not for too long. Alec doesn't want to have to supercleanse himself for the third time this week, although he knows he will probably have to anyway after the walk they take after dinner.

Yesterday, Alec went to the store to purchase a newspaper, since the paper wasn't delivered and his mother wanted him to get it as soon as possible. When he was walking to the store to purchase the newspaper, a man brushed Alec's shirt with his shirt as he walked by. Alec almost yelled out, "You contaminated me! You poisoned me! Come back here and get rid of your filthy poison!" He almost turned around and went back home and recleansed, but he was right outside the store. So he continued: he would be contaminated again anyway when he'd touch the money and when he'd touch the paper. Someone else always touches the newspaper. Then he'd have to supercleanse himself again.

"I would like to go to a restaurant and eat there and listen to nice quiet music while we eat," he says. He thinks he can smell his mother's smell on the receiver, and he holds it further from his mouth. There could be worse smells, but it is still contaminated.

"Oh, okay," Cara says. Alec likes this way of talking, where not too much is said, where he doesn't have to listen to too many things that he doesn't want to listen to. He likes to keep things simple. Who needs to think? Alec can talk like this with Cara for the rest of the night. Forget about food and music. Forget about the walk. Just talk about simple things.

"You know, I was wondering," Cara says. Alec doesn't like this sudden tone. He doesn't want her wondering, or thinking at all. If she can't help it, she can think, but he wants her to keep it to herself. "You must be really smart to have all those degrees. Because I'm just starting, you know, and I can tell it's going to be a real challenge to finish for me. I mean, it's college and all."

"Uh-huh," Alec says. Alec wants to hang up the phone. He pulls his ear further from the receiver. The more he thinks about it, the more he doesn't know exactly why he is talking to this person. He has told her lies by not telling her more about himself. He didn't tell her he went to a graduate school and Ph.D. program that he created. He didn't tell her he was his own advisor, or that he created his own program, read what he put on his own syllabuses, wrote his own essays, and turned them in to himself, mostly on time. He didn't tell her he gave himself a solid 3.73 GPA, or that he just finished his own thesis, since his committee of himself didn't pass himself on the first try. Alec didn't tell her any of this.

"I want you to tell me more about you," Cara says.

"Uh-huh," Alec said. "I will see you then." He hangs up the phone and walks to the bathroom. He must recleanse before he leaves for his date. The phone rings again.

"Oh, Cara," he says. "Hello. How nice of you to call again," he says.

"When – I was just, you know, wondering – are we meeting exactly?" she asks. "And what restaurant were you talking about?"

Alec hasn't had sexual relations with a woman, but he knows all about it. He knows what you need to do to a woman in bed. Or at least he has some good ideas from television. Alec is already married though. He married himself last spring in a grand ritual in the backyard, under the sycamore tree with the birds and squirrels skittering and chirping. He held his own hand and made the vows to himself. If he has sexual relations with Cara or any other woman, not only will he corrupt his being, but he will be cheating on himself – and then he will be jealous of himself. But Alec can't help his thoughts. His thoughts run amuck, and for that he has to pay penance. Alec can find another way to compensate.

After he married himself, he came up with the idea. He would write a book springing from his thesis, the innate Darwinian value of misogyny to the success of the male species throughout the history of civilization. The book would be partially a glimpse into the lives of famous misogynists – a sort of homage to past masters – as well as a defense of misogyny itself. As he thought about the project more, Alec knew he would write a *Devil's Dictionary* of misogyny, an ABC's of precisely how and why to hate women. He decided to find work at the community college last week. This was not so much for the job though – it was for his fieldwork. He could get to know some real live women there and watch them operate in the real world. He could make notes and observations. He could find examples of contemporary womanhood. He had to find out what it was like to be a woman today before he could justify his book, which he knew he would call *The Misogynist's Handbook*.

The problem was nobody believed his credentials. He tried to tell them that he finished his masters and the committee just approved his Ph.D., but when they asked where he did his work, he wasn't going to lie. Not for this. He wanted to get the job on his own merits.

The secretary at the community college yawned, squinted her eyes, and fingered the ebony brooch pinned under the shoulder of her cardigan.

"My house. My own program in social history, actually."

"I don't understand," the secretary said.

"I worked on my thesis by myself. It was all self-oriented," Alec said. He stood in front of her as straight as possible. He clasped his hands behind his back. This seemed to be a professional stance. "I am a very intelligent, yet self-effacing man."

"I see," the secretary said. "So there wasn't a university to sponsor you? You didn't actually go to a university. You just read to yourself?" Her eyes flashed, then became jittery and spooked.

"No," Alec said. "I wanted to do it by myself."

"But sir, you must, you know, you must have an accredited master's degree to seek employment here," the secretary said. She shuffled papers on her desk.

"I did the work," he said. "You can read my thesis. Can I please fill out an application? I am already feeling debased by this conversation, and I'd like to leave as soon as possible."

"I see," the secretary said, and glanced at her phone. Alec thought her nervous gestures made her look like a parakeet. She looked over her shoulder. Alec knew she was trying to make sure her colleagues were still in the area. He could tell she didn't know what to make of him. This was to be expected, he thought.

"Why don't you just fill out an application," she said, handing Alec the form. He listened as she called security, but he didn't expect them to actually approach him in the office.

"Why don't you fly away now?" Alec told her. "Flap your wings and flutter, birdy woman." The secretary walked out of the reception area, into a room in back.

The security guard tapped him on the shoulder. "Why don't we go on home now," the man said. He was a droopy puppy-dog man, a natural protector. His eyes were lost.

"I need to finish filling out the application," Alec said. "And then I will go home and decontaminate."

"No, we need to go now," the man said. Alec put up a fight, pushing the droopy man and angering him, and forcing the man to find other security guards to escort Alec from the campus, shoving him into the woods.

As he walked from the campus into the woods surrounding the area, he saw a girl walking toward him along the path that leads to the college. He walked by the girl, and the girl watched him and watched him.

"Are you trying to find the campus?" the girl asked. Alec turned around in the woods. He could hear the birds chatter in the trees, and the squirrels skitter in the leaves. These things calmed him.

"No," Alec said, looking at her. She was short but not too short, with dark brown hair that wasn't too brown, and olivey-tan skin that glistened. She was a thing of beauty, Alec thought. That hair was what caught his eye the most. He had to touch that hair. He wanted to be able to touch that hair anytime, anywhere. He wanted to hold the hair in his hands and press it to his face. "I was trying to find you."

"Me?" she said. "I've never... Do I know you?"

"No," Alec said. "But you are a thing of beauty. You have beautiful brown hair, and your voice is a little you that comes out and crawls in your ear and makes me feel better."

"Oh," she said, and put her hand over her mouth. "Wow."

"Can I take you on a romantic date?" Alec asked.

"I'm not sure," she said. "I'm a bit out of breath here." But she laughed and gave him her phone number, and said he should call, and when he watched her walk away, she turned around several times and smiled. This is a good sign, Alec thought. Alec decided to smile back, and pretend to be nice, and just be goofy and young, and then he walked home to supercleanse.

*

RANTS AND RAVES

That evening Alec brainstormed in his notebook. "I wish it was that simple to say that rape is about power," he wrote. "Mostly rape is a product of the woman's seductive power of being, which is to say that it is justified by man's being. Men should be able to take what they want. Moreover, they will anyway. You can't restrain the male libido, as you can't dam the Pacific Ocean." And then he wrote, "In the West polygamy will be and should be resuscitated in this century to follow the natural order of the Old Testament." And then he wrote: "A reason to hate women: their need to follow the dictates of society. Men are the only true innovators."

Then his mother called him for dinner, and they sat together in silence and ate the pot roast and potatoes. The only words they spoke were "pass the salt please," and "can I have the pepper?" Alec loves his mother. She lets him be, and she doesn't bother him when he's thinking, and doesn't talk to him too much or distract him. She doesn't care what he does, and she doesn't pressure him to do anything in particular. She listens when he quotes Samuel Johnson on the vileness of the feminine will. She makes her quilts and crochets, and sits and watches violent police shows on television with him. When Alec is with his mother, he thinks: this is nice, this is the way it should be. Watching violent police shows. Speaking my mind. Alec doesn't think of her as a woman like these other types. He thinks of his mother as different and special above and beyond the fray.

Alec walks into the Italian restaurant and sees Cara already sitting underneath a fake trellis with fake ivy running up the fake wood. He arrives twenty-five minutes late on purpose so he can see if she is devoted to him, and she is. No complaints. He stands in front of her and he takes her hand and kisses it, and sits down across from her and hands her a box. She smiles and opens the box, and inside is a clump of his curly hair. At first she laughs, but then she presses her hands together, and closes the box on the table and wants to know why he gave her this.

"Don't get scared," Alec says. "Let me explain. I'm giving you hair as a sign of interest. I'm giving you a part of myself right now. And later, if we develop according to normal male-female relations,

I will give you other parts of myself. This is a start. Hair is just a signal."

"Oh," she says. Cara's hands clasp the edge of the restaurant table and her fingernails dig into the tablecloth. Her fingernails are painted a light pink with a tinge of lavender. She smells of rosemary. Alec notices her earrings are turquoise, and that her pink fingernails are slightly chipped, and that a fine fuzz of hair is visible above her lip. But just barely. His mother has thin fuzz like that also, Alec thinks. Sometimes Alec dreams of his mother watching violent cop shows on television with him. In the dream they'll sit in the dark and watch the cops shoot people, and watch the other people shoot the cops. Just like real life. Alec needs the routine, and if he didn't step outside his own reality and contaminate himself sometimes, he would forget how pure his own reality is, and what contamination is in the first place. This is why he's here, he thinks. Violence and sex and depravity are useful to instill in him a sense of purity. Then he will pray, and then he will do penance to rid himself of these thoughts. This is part of the cleansing process.

"It's healthy hair," he says. "I just washed it."

"Look," she says. "What is all this about really?" She seems like an upset babysitter. Alec wonders if she's about to scold him.

"I don't understand," he says. "I wanted to take you on a romantic date. I wanted to treat you right, like the knights used to do. That's the way it should be."

"Oh," she says. "But why?"

"The truth is," he says, "I'm interested in you. But I am new to this business of dating. I am new to women, but I am curious about the female species. I'm also writing a book. I'm studying you, among other things."

"You are curious about me?" she asks.

"I am very curious," he says. "I am curious about a lot of things. But most of all I'm curious about you." And Alec proceeds to tell her all about the types of weather he likes and dislikes, about the neighborhood where he lives, about his college days at a mostly all-girls school, and about his post-college days of self-instruction: six years of intense study and writing. He doesn't want to tell her too much. He doesn't want to tell her about the project. She smiles and says she has weather that she dislikes too. She seems like a nice, normal girl. She asks about his book, and he says it's about different types of weather and how they make him feel.

"People like to read about weather," he says. "People don't like to think nearly as much as some people say they do."

Mostly, Alec doesn't want to ask about her. He doesn't want to know about her at all. He wants her to sit there across from him and look pretty and listen to him. This is what she should do. Just be a mirror for what he says. Reflect. Reflect.

The waitress approaches them and they order dinner, and Alec orders a bottle of wine for Cara. Cara drinks a glass of wine and Alec asks her to drink another. Cara runs her thumb up and down the stem of the wine glass, and Alec notices the trail of oil from her fingers when they withdraw.

After dinner, Alec and Cara walk around the man-made lake. There are no real lakes in this whole state, he knows. This makes it even better. He doesn't touch her hand. He doesn't touch her shoulders. Alec walks slightly behind her, so he can watch the muscles in her jaw and neck, so he can watch her hair bob as she walks. He watches the way she turns her neck to look at him, and how her hair turns with her head. She tries to tell him about her childhood, her hopes and dreams, but he raises his finger and tells her to be quiet, because there might be rapists and evildoers in the woods.

"There might be robbers hiding in the woods," he says. "You never know. There might be evil demons in the night, lurking and waiting to hear you talk about your hopes and dreams."

"Right," she says with a slight chuckle. "You're so ironic."

Cara reaches out to hold his hand and walk closer to him, but Alec puts his hands in his pockets. Alec desires to stick his fingers in her vagina, right here in the woods, sitting next to the lake, listening to the water lap against the shore. Alec thinks he can do such a thing if he wants to and she will acquiesce because that's what women are good at doing. He knows he can take off her blouse and touch her breasts if he wants to. He wonders what breasts feel like. He can put her hand on his penis if he wants to, and he can make her do things down there. If he wants, he can hold her hair in a ponytail like a leash and make her do other things down there. At least, these are things he's seen on television.

Yet Alec knows he is better than that. He doesn't need to slouch in sin to feel alive. He doesn't have to weaken his will like women do. Instead, Alec reaches over and puts his hand on Cara's forehead.

"Can I have some of your hair?" he asks.

"That's a good one," she says. "That reminds me—"

"I'm serious," he says. Alec clasps his hands behind his back and bends his neck over her. He is impressed by his own power. He knows he can overwhelm her if he wants to. Alec is bigger and stronger, and he knows he can have his way. He likes this feeling. He likes feeling stronger than Cara, and for a moment this feeling wells up in him as if it might take control of his entire body.

"What? I don't think so," she says. "I'm pretty sure we have enough hair floating around for this evening."

Alec takes the scissors out of his pocket and holds them in front of her so she can see them.

"What are you doing?" She stops in the path.

"I just want some of your hair," he says. "I want something to remember this beautiful romantic evening by. Hair seems perfect to me."

Cara starts to back away, but Alec catches her by the hand. He has to have a lock of her hair so he can build a shrine, so he can put some of her hair in a plastic case and look at it and touch it, and touch himself and smell the hair as he touches himself all over. He may never see her again, he thinks, but at least he will have some of her beautiful brown-but-not-too-brown hair. She will have his, and he will have hers. They will have shared this together.

Cara tells him to let her go. She says she wants to go. She says no. She screams. Cara screams as loud as she can, but Alec clips into the thick mane of her hair and lifts a lock of hair from the mass, and folds the lock into his pocket. Cara yells for help and pushes him away, and then Alec lets her go. Alec watches her run down the path into the dark, and Alec can hear her footsteps recede through the dark.

*

RANTS AND RAVES

When Alec returns home, he drops the lock of Cara's hair into his plastic case. He writes in his notebook: "The vanity of women is ceaseless. They are unable to give of themselves as men can. They are unable to be courageous and reveal themselves to men. Men are the only true honest creatures."

Alec walks to the linen closet and takes four towels from his stack of white towels, and enters the bathroom. He closes the door quietly behind him, careful to not wake his mother. She has her chemo tomorrow, and needs to rest. Alec knows he will have to find another object of study now. But perhaps this is how it should be. It was a good first step, but Cara wasn't the right one. His perfect object of study must be a woman who likes the hair idea. Cara wasn't committed, he thinks. But there are so many out there, just waiting for him. Alec knows he will have to search and search until he finds the right one. And it will be done.

DROSS

I watch it fill with breath. I watch it rise and fall. I pray for the day when she groans in the bathroom, releasing the bloody clod, the mouse head slipping through the sewer line – the fish tail, the chicken body, the unbaked cookie bobbing in the bowl. If He will only grace me.
    I can taste my own bile in my throat. Eggy. Sour. I nauseate myself. I watch the downy hairs on her arms whistle in the air-conditioning like wheat stalks. Her skin is thin and pliable. I can see her veins through her pale skin. I watch the skin on her stomach working like soft and gentle bellows. Blowing. Blowing. I am fully dressed and alert. Sweat dribbles down my side.
    Our bedroom smells of lilac and potpourri and cinnamon. She has scented the air with candles for her blooming. I hear the scratch of leaves and branches against the siding. I hear crickets in the underbrush. I can see the glow from the softball field lights through the branches and leaves. Our children are asleep, but I can feel a writhing around me. They are snakes in a basket. The snakes are alive and writhing. I'm fully dressed and alert. I'm standing over her in my sweatshirt. My hood is heavy against my shoulder blades. The strings from the hood bob and bob. I'm shivering. My hands won't stop. He will come to me tonight.
    I imagine the impact in slow motion. My fist careens from the shadows above, collapsing into the taut rising and falling, the force jolting her out of her slumber, her eyes bugged, the mouse head's little chicken body crushed by the blow, the uterus quaking in the pain of expulsion. I listen to the hum of the air-conditioning. Headlights pan across the room. A smell of exhaust. A muffler rattles. The car slows. The car turns into our driveway and backs out. I wish I were headed in the other direction.
    I have nine children. My wife will not restrain. She will not *allow* for restraint. My wife is a woman of the Lord. I am a man of the

Lord. We spend our money on food and clothing for the children. I drive our nine children in a twelve-year-old black van. My children wear clothes from Goodwill, and hand-me-downs from my brothers. I haven't been on a vacation for fifteen years. One mistake is all you get. Then you offer your life in exchange for diapers and pacifiers, cream of spinach baby food and more diapers, pampers, safety pins, booties, sockies, hatties, blocks, games, plastic horsies, plastic elephants, stuffed animals, slush puppies, car seats, figure-skating practice, video-game systems, dirt bikes, tennis shoes, scrunchies, mittens, sleds, backpacks, graphing calculators, Barbie dolls, Matchbox cars, more plastic horsies, more sockies and hatties. I walk out of the lilac, and into the shadows of the corridor towards my children's rooms. My arms are stiff at my sides. My fingernails leave marks on the flesh of my palms.

Yesterday the four men came again. Yet they were one. They had their wings, and their four faces, and their violent amber, and their legs. Their wings were joined, and they were one. The lion faces gave me a solemn look. The ox faces mewed solemnly. The eagle faces gestured to me with their beaks. The men faces were blank. They were on fire as they spoke, like burnished brass. The amber sparked at me like fire, and then they were fire. Their feet were like calves feet. Their amber hair was covered with eyes. They spoke without speaking. My body was as light as dust, and heavy as a mountain. My mind was filled but empty. I felt nauseous. I awoke pasty with my own vomit.

When I awoke, I remembered. He told me again. He told me I must preserve my line at any cost. He commanded me: I must not abandon the family to serve myself. My needs are always second. My duty is the whole. My duty is to serve this line, and to increase this line, for nobody but I can do this. "Lord," I said. "I pray to You, Lord," I said. "I pray to You to offer me another duty. This duty will be my ruin."

He said there is no other duty for me. He said this is my duty. He said this is what He asks of me. He speaks to me and me alone. I am cursed. I am cursed. He seduces and rapes me. He bashes my head with His will. He molds my mind with His will.

"Lord, I beg of You," I said. "You have given me boils. You have given me ulcers and wracked my body with labor. I beg of You. I cannot do what You ask of me. I beg You for another duty."

He said my duty is to serve this line, this family. He said my duty is to protect and destroy in turn, in service of this line. He said my duty is to purify what is and what is to be. He will have more to ask of me. He said He has much for me to do, and that I must gain strength for the battle that must be waged.

To save my line I must go to the infant Hal and change him. This is of immense importance, He said. "Poor Hal has been sick," I said. "What can I do?" Once I have the dirty diaper, He said I must lay the soiled cloth flat. When the cloth is flat, I must press my face into Hal's shit. When I press my face into Hal's shit, I must inhale the shit and eat the shit. If I taste and smell pneumonia in the shit, I must take him to the hospital. If I taste pneumonia, she can no longer produce. If I taste pneumonia, the baby will be born without legs. If I taste pneumonia, the baby will be born with a mouse head. If I taste pneumonia, she must lose what she carries. That life must be taken from her, for it will ruin the line.

"Lord, how will I know if I taste pneumonia? How can you taste an affliction, Lord?"

I awoke knowing that I would know if it was indeed pneumonia. I would know.

I did as he asked. I found the diaper as he commanded. I opened the diaper and I pressed my face into it. I smelled and ate the shit. I smelled and tasted the pneumonia. He guided me. He is the truth. He is Truth. I vomited and washed my face in the sink, and washed the vomit and the water down the drain of the sink. I drove Hal to the hospital, and he will be fine, they say. He will live. One more day and we can pick him up. They need to keep watch.

I leave her and walk down the corridor. I will sleep in the van tonight. I am a danger to my family. Yet I must do what He commanded. I must make good on His word. Hal has pneumonia, and he sleeps in the hospital, and I must make good on His word. But first I must gain strength. First I must rest.

I walk downstairs and open the room where my boys sleep. I can smell their young sweat. I can hear their soft exhales. None of the boys stir. I train them to box. They can play football. Their muscles are taut. Their little legs are strong. Warriors. Their little bodies will fill into my shoes someday. Their shoes will carry bodies that will outlive me. Their little bodies will carry this line. There is no need to walk into the girls' room. They give me boils and ulcers. I imagine throwing them in the murk. They would flail and sink into the eels and sludge. He does not command me to imagine this. I imagine this regardless. They consume and will give nothing back to the line. They are deadweight. As I walk past their room, I bump their door. Perhaps they will wake. I hope they have a restless sleep. I have boils on my hands and feet. I can feel my boils chaffing against my socks. My ulcer gnashes its teeth. I have to sit down on the stairs until it passes.

I will sleep in the van in the driveway. I go to the kitchen and get the twine. I go to the sofa and get a pillow. I step outside and lock and door, and I certainly have my gun. I place the gun in the glove compartment. Nobody will come and soil my line. I wrap myself in the twine and tie it around my arms. I will not allow myself to do His will tonight. I will rest. I will rest. I lay the pillow on the seat of the van and I lay my head on it, and I sleep.

In my dream He came to me and spoke. He told me He was furious. He said I have not followed his advice. I told him of the baby Hal and what I discovered and what I did. He wanted action for the future.

He said the future of the line depends on my actions tomorrow. He was in a fury. His faces whirled and burned in fire. He was a whirlwind. He was filled with vengeance. He said if I could not follow his word, He would impose his word. How is this possible? How is this possible? Lord, why? Lord, don't afflict me. Lord, give me my due time.

I awake and undo my bonds. I enter sounds. Clinking and clanking. The sounds of food and drink. We built my oldest an apartment in the basement. Hank has returned with a woman, Glenda. They argue about jelly and sugar cane. In the kitchen and dining room are

Sylvie, and Hanna, and Mary. There is Kyle, and Edward, and Jeremy. There is Katie, and Valerie. They eat. They drink. They walk and garble words to each other, and to Hank and Glenda, and their mother. There is orange juice and milk and biscuits. The noise overwhelms me. All I hear is the whole. Clattering and clinking. Chewing and spilling.

My children have suspect eyes. Mary has a lazy eye. Kyle has the eyes of cats. Sylvie has raven eyes. They all have eyes up to no good at all. I have given life to evil eyes. There is the sound of the television and the sound of the radio. I wail against it, but she tells me that she must have her necessities. I tell her we have our necessities. She *wants* the image. She *wants* the sound. I cover my ears and whisk myself through to the bedroom. Lord, I am paying for my sins. I am praying for the sins of my line. I am praying for the sins of the screen and the sounds. When we were young, I sinned. Now I fantasize of sin. I pray for the end to fantasy. Lord, I am lost. Give me guidance. I will atone one a day at a time. I beg You, let me have my life. Now my life is their life.

We live near the river. When I was a boy, my happiest moments were on the river. I loved the brown sludge. I loved the eels, and the bluegills. I would bash the bluegills with my oar and sprinkle salt over them, and eat them raw in the middle of the river. I would bite the head from the eels and eat them. I would eat their essence, their animalness. Two minutes prior it was alive. Two minutes prior the animal was swimming, thinking, shitting, eating. Then it is being destroyed by something larger than it could imagine. We learn humbleness too late. I would eat oranges and potato chips with those fish and eels. I would trail my hands in the brown sludge and wipe the blood from my hands on the side of the boat. I would watch the blood wash from the boat as I rowed away through the sludge.

My mother asked me why I never returned with fish. I told her I wasn't a good fisherman. I wonder if she saw blood on my teeth, or scales on my lips. My father asked me if I thought I was a sensible kid. I told him I wasn't. He looked at me with distrust. I looked at him with my youthful peace. I felt controlled even then. I didn't know what pulled the strings, but I knew the strings hung from me. I didn't need the same things as other kids, I told him. That's why

I'm not sensible, I told him. He said I was sensible because I was his son. As if blood alone would make me sensible. They never looked at the red heels of the oars or the worn oarlocks. Then they would have known me better. They were *adults*. They accepted as is.

Last month I saw an old friend. William is a civil engineer downtown. He's working on the new twelve-lane bridge. He lives alone in a townhouse. He told me he hadn't been with a woman in two years. He hasn't even touched himself. His life is and was the creation of this bridge. All his energy was devoted to the construction. He didn't have time for destruction, he said. He didn't have time for the senses. He is tall and lean, hair cropped to his skull like an extra skin. He smells like leather. Was he once part of my thoughts? He is outside of me.

"I envy you," I said. "I envy everything you have, but also everything you don't have. That's the more important part."

"There is nothing to envy," he said. "My life is simple. I try to keep it stream-lined."

"That is what I envy," I said.

I like to split wood. I like to build. I studied architecture, but I can't... I can't produce. I can't create. I can only fulfill what *is* already. I want to be an architect. I want to have a fertile mind. But it is not in His plan. He wants me to edit trade magazines. I live in the word and the word domineers me. I live for God and God denies me. I live the word and the word shits on me.

I'm in the backyard. The dogs are pacing inside the fence. I can hear their fur brush against the wooden enclosure. I can hear their panting breath. They smell of piss and mud. They disgust me. She wants them to guard. I want the gun. I tell her we don't need both. The enclosure is rotting. I can smell the splinters.

I chop wood. I have a chopping block. I have a wedge and a sledgehammer. With each blow the dogs bark. With each blow the windows shudder. With each blow my body is more mine, and more His. I split wood for the wood stove that heats the basement. I will edit in the basement near the fire and warm myself. The fire will give me energy to work. In the end the cold will eat the warm. In the end the son will eat the father. The father will pass and wheat will spring from his bones and the son's sons will eat the wheat and the son's sons will eat them. This is the way. We are all consumed. I must maintain the line. Tttttttttt. Tttttttttt. Tttttttttt. Tttttttttt. The dogs grumble.

I place one of the logs against the fence and stand upon it, and peer over the fence. The bitch leaps up to bite me. Their pen is littered with shit and stagnant pools of piss. Their fur is matted. Ruts litter the mud. The dogs lick each other and eat each other's shit and piss. How can these protect us? Lord, how can these creatures comfort us? Lord, what course of action should I take? Lord, must I live in my own containment?

I light the fire with rags and kindling. The wood burns true and warms me. I can hear the feet above me. My children run and scream. I can hear heavy objects falling. I hear things breaking. I hear the screen. I hear the sounds. I am reading an article on the glass used in the new airport. The author has control of the subject, but she can't write. I tear into the article with my red pen. I slash adverbs and adjectives. I simplify the cumbersome sentences. I restructure the paragraphs. I streamline.

The fire is warm. I feel sleepy. My skin burns from the twine. I decide to shower, but to shower I must go upstairs. That I won't do. We didn't want them to learn the unholy. We wanted them to learn the ways of God. We wanted them to learn right. Yet I can't walk in my own house. I am an imposition in my own life. I decide not to shower.

I went camping in February. My mother owns a parcel of land in Frederick County. It used to be a farm. Now it's nothing but woods. Her brothers used to hunt there. When I need to get away, that's where I go. When my mother passes, I will get the land. When I get the land, I will build a house upon it and live on the fruits of the land. They say she has three months.

It was twenty-six during the day. It was zero at night. I wore five layers of clothes and two pairs of gloves and two hats and two coats, and I slept in the thermal sleeping bag and ate canned potatoes and

sauerkraut. It snowed on the first night. I had to heat my frozen drinking water. During the day, I watched deer eat springs from the trees.
    I thought. I regretted. I lamented the role that she plays in my life, and the path I agreed to go down. When we had Hank, we would hike with him on my back. We talked about the future then. When we talked about it, I told her I wanted to be at home with the children. I told her I wanted to be domestic. I told her I wanted to be around. That's what she wanted also. My mother can support us. My mother needs to feel needed.
    I walked through the snow. I watched the stately winter sky. I watched the cirrus clouds and the space between the clouds. The space between the clouds was what caught my interest.

When I open my eyes, the fire is a brown smudge. She is standing next to me. I hate Labor Day. Everything turns to shit on Labor Day. She stands over me when I wake up. Her hands are heavy on my shoulders. Her fingernails nick my skin. I can smell her. Her smell. She clears her throat. I can hear the children. I can hear footsteps above me.
    "The dogs escaped," she says.
    Labor Day 1988: got in a car accident. Labor Day 1989: Mary got the chicken pox. Labor Day 1991: big fight. Labor Day 1992: refrigerator broke. Labor Day 1993: Mother had a stroke. Labor Day 1995: house broken into. Labor Day 1996: Edward broke his arm. Labor Day 1997: I got pneumonia. Labor Day 1998: pneumonia. Labor Day 1999: more pneumonia. Labor Day 2000: the dogs escape.
    "Edward," I say. "Edward can find them," I say. "Mary will help." I have work to do. I must start another fire. I am tired of smelling her passivity.
    "Yes," she says. "It will be done."
    She is passivity. She is helplessness. She is complete abandonment. We play the game and lose. They seduce us into these lives where they garner power. They are in control within these matrimonial lives. The gateway has been closed years ago. Our vows seduced me. I am a bound man, and I hate her for it. I hate her

single-mindedness. I hate her fearless drive to produce. I hate her domesticity. I hate her organs. She has claimed what I own as hers. She has claimed my innards.

I see Richard. Richard is my oldest and wisest friend. We went to high school together. In high school we were inseparable. He has a heart. He has an inner life. He is a musician. He plays second violin for the BSO. He resents his position. I drink orange juice in his living room. His birds chatter in the kitchen. He knows not to turn on the screen.

"We all have unfulfilled desires," he says. "I wanted to play in the next Led Zeppelin. I wanted to hop around on stage with hair down to my ass, but that was impossible."

Richard speaks in an even, measured tone. His even and measured tone relaxes me. His orange juice relaxes me. He offers me weed. I decline the weed. He offers me vodka. I decline the vodka. He offers me heroin. I decline the heroin.

"I know," I say. "But I'm wasting my talents. I'm intelligent. I can make contributions to society."

"Yes," he says. "You can."

"I could do a lot of things if I was in a different situation."

"True," he says. "But you wouldn't have the children. You wouldn't have the wife."

"That's what I'm saying," I say. "I want to do what I studied. I want to be an architect. I want to create."

"And you wouldn't miss them?"

"Right now, no. Honestly, no," I say.

"Yet, if you lived in this alternate universe, you would think differently. You might long for a wife and children," he says.

"No, I don't think so," I say.

"You don't think so," he says.

"Don't minimize this," I say. "Richard, don't tell me what I think and don't think. I'm telling you what I think right now."

"You want some more orange juice," he says.

"Fine," I say. I watch him pour the orange juice. The birds watch me drink the orange juice. In his kitchen he has a poster of a clipper ship. Imprinted underneath the ship in red bubble letters the poster reads: "A ship in port is safe, but that's not what ships are built for." The word becomes flesh.

I want to get drunk and fuck unknown women. You hear about this. Nobody does these things. Today I go to a bar to do these things.
    At the bar, most of the people watch the game on the television. I look up at the television and I can't concentrate. I can't see order. I see the colors. I hear the sounds. I can't piece it all together. I sit by the door and stare out the window. The window is streaked with mud. For once it's not raining out. A man stares at the television. He circles his finger on the wet counter. His eyes are red. He lifts his wet fingers to his mouth. He doesn't blink.
    When a woman enters the bar, I pretend to tip my cap. I say something cute: "You are a sweet young thing." I hear the ladies like that. These ladies don't. These ladies squint at me or ignore me. One woman looks like she wants to smack me, but she doesn't. It's okay, because the ladies aren't pretty. I lie. I want to fuck the unpretty women.
    What I'd like to do afterwards is talk about what *I* want to talk about. *I* get to set the agenda. We won't be talking about Mary's booster shots, or Hal. I'd like a lady to lie next to me and listen to me talk about how my squadron of children is eating me out of house and home like a swarm of locusts. And the missing dogs. I'd tell her how God hounds me with His prophecies, how He makes demands of me, how He burdens me. I'd tell her about the dreams. She'd tell me she wanted to fuck me again, and she'd lick me all over. She'd say sweet sexy things. I'd want to make her lick my feet, but I wouldn't. I'd be nice.
    The seat by the bar isn't working. The ladies seem to be able to see my wedding ring right through my pocket. I start being more honest. A lady enters the bar. I tell her my wife doesn't let me masturbate. I tell her my wife makes me clean my spilled seed with my face. I tell her my wife only has sex for procreation. I have to follow her around and around and around around and around the bar to tell her. The colors swirl. The sounds. I throw bottles at the screen. I throw ashtrays at the screen. The bar jostles. I am pushed out. I stumble into mulch, lean against a tree.

*

By the time I return it's eight. We have dinner at seven. She tells me I smell like smoke and beer. I tell her that lots of people are burning fires.
"It's Labor Day," she says. "It's not cold."
She doesn't understand need.
She hands me a plate. On the plate are mashed potatoes, liver, green beans, and artichoke hearts. How does she find time to cook these things? How does she find time to think? How does she find time to breathe? She is a machine. I watch her stomach rise and fall with breath. Her diaphragm inhales and exhales. I think of the knives. I think of the pots and pans. She is saying something, but I can't hear her. I am thinking of what I must do.
The room is empty as I eat. As I eat, I can hear my own chewing. The basket of snakes writhes in the walls, but it is silent. I can hear my teeth. I can hear my tongue. I can hear my mouth wash the food down with water. I can hear the river. I can hear a heron's cry across the river. I can also hear an egret. Their cries form one cry.

I help in getting them to bed. I read them stories. I talk to them about their bad dreams. I tell them I have bad dreams too. I tuck them into their covers and turn on night lights. Yes, I say, even adults have bad dreams. Dreams never leave you, I say. Dreams stay with you more than what really happens. That's why they're scary. Sure, I'll be right in the room if you need me, I say. Everything's going to be just fine.
I sit in the hall and read a book to let them know I'm there. They can see my legs from their rooms. Sylvie comes and sits with me and I rub her back. That always works. Katie comes and sits with me and I scratch her back. I carry them back to their beds, and they sleep.
My wife tells me she'd like me to come to bed. She is framed by the darkness behind her. Her face is the color of parchment.
I decide to tell her about my trip to the bar. She laughs at me. She tells me she is disgusted by me. She sleeps on her side. I lie in bed in the dark, looking at her back. Her back is an ominous wall. I can't see her stomach rise and fall. I am distracted. He will present

Himself and say I am weak. He will question me and give me sores and worse. I'm exhausted. I can't summon the energy. I drift off.

In my dream He comes in the form of four. The wings beat angrily, and they are wings of fire. The legs paw the ground. It is cold and I shiver in the chill, but I can only see my breath, and the amber fire, and the wings, and the many faces and eyes. I am subsumed. He asks me to turn behind me and look. I do. I turn slowly, and I'm terrified. I close my eyes. I can hear the angry wings behind me. Fffffffffffffffffffffff. Fffffffffffffffffffffffffffffff. Ffffffffffffffffffffff.

I open my eyes, and there is a table illuminated in light. On the table is a single book. He tells me to pick up the book and turn around to face Him. I pick up the book and turn and as I turn the wings beat faster and faster until I can no longer discern the beating of the wings from each other. I am completely surrounded, and He is no longer the four. He is a whirlwind. He is the air. He is everywhere. He is nowhere. He speaks. He says I must eat the book. The book is my life and I know it already. He says I must do as He commanded before. He says the child cannot live. And I am weak. I need strength. To get strength I must eat the book. I must eat each page and the cover. I do. I eat the book and the cover, and it tastes like a sweet fruit. It tastes like a tropical delicacy. It is not unpleasant.

As I ingest the pages, He commands me to destroy the falseness in my home. We have false idols in my home, and they must be destroyed. I know what they are. I have seen the screens, I tell him. I have seen what is on the screens. I have heard the sounds from the radio and the screens.

"I will, my Lord," I say. We have images of greed and vanity and hatred commanding our children, He says. We have images of lust and deceit throughout our home. They must be destroyed. "I will, my Lord," I say. These commands must be followed, He says. "I will, my Lord."

I awake to the sound of lawnmowers and the syrupy hum of early morning birds. I can hear my wife and children in the kitchen. I blink in the morning sunlight. The sky is clear. The trees sway in the wind.

I watch the limbs sway. The shadows sway into the room. The sky feels close. The curtains are flimsy. The valance is thin. I lift my head, and my mind is settled. He has seduced and raped me. I am awed. I am taken. I am ready. I am ready to do what I must. I rise into the morning. I step into the light.

The Ballad of Ted and Maddie

Amy

She, like, became friends with this old guy because he came up to her at this neighborhood cook-out thing, and he told her he went to Fordham High too (the class of '86 or something), and that she looks a lot like a girl he used to date back then, and then he gave her a piece of his barbequed chicken, or a rib or something, and she said he was sweet and kinda handsome for an older man (I think that's what she said), and I think she had her softball jersey on, buttons halfway down. I can see her. She was probably trying to stick them out for him, and who knows what else, because that's what Maddie does now. She tries to lure them in. Maddie didn't use to be flirty or, like, a total tart or anything, but all that's changed now.

    At first she didn't make it sound like anything weird, not like he was going to get her shit-faced drunk and molest her in the woods or something, but I have to admit I was worried as soon as she told me about him. I kept thinking, it's just not regular. This isn't what people do. But I kept my mouth shut, because to me friends are really just for listening and being with, and if she, like, wanted my opinion or something, she'd ask for it, right?

    Of course, Maddie told me all about him. He worked as a counselor for older people – like, helping them cope with death and stuff, making their stay at the home easier, and that kind of thing – and he loved to be outside doing this and that, like sailing out on the bay and chopping down big trees. And he spent a lot of time at work giving drugs to these old people, and giving them shots, and he was kinda depressed, and he had a lot of his clients die 'cause they *are* old – I mean, you know – and his name was Ted. And he *was* tall and handsome, I have to admit, with this bristly black hair like a horse, and long arms like that guy in the Guinness Book who could like tie his own knee stockings without bending over. I'm not exaggerating.

But the thing that Maddie talked about most was Ted's hands. She had never seen hands like these. Like, they were large and soft and hard at the same time, like dough or something, or like the biscuits my mom makes, and they were hard and callused, since maybe he had blisters all the time when he was younger or something, or since maybe he was a lumberjack or used to beat people up all the time or something. I know he was a construction worker at one point. I know that 'cause he told me he was soooooo, like, proud of the time when he used to work with his hands, as if it was such a big deal. I mean, everybody has hands. Even monkeys. But it was, like, one of the first things he told me. After college for a couple years he lived in New Mexico, and he made sure I knew it wasn't on a commune with a bunch of hippies or anything queer like that. It was about building houses and sleeping under the stars, all that macho crap.

It's funny, when Ted talked, he always spent a lot of time making sure I didn't think anything was wrong. But I saw things. For example: I knew he didn't love his wife. He lived with his Korean wife, Sung, who was really pretty and all that, and she was a good cook, and she helped him deal with things, I guess, but they didn't have kids of their own and they never would, Maddie told me. She didn't say why, but I had some guesses. He looked at his wife like she was just another person who happened to be around. Not like she was something special. There was, like, no glimmer in his eyes. And she seemed like she had all kinds of other things in her head that she wasn't saying to anybody. But then, what do you expect when you get past twenty-five?

So Ted started having Maddie over for dinner, and to watch movies and stuff like that, stuff that Maddie would do with me or her other friends before he came along. She started going over there basically every night, and she basically stopped calling me. That was Maddie's deal, and no matter what anybody says, that's why we're not friends anymore. She's, like, an excluder. Every time a boy would come along, she'd forget about all of us, like she was better than us 'cause she had a boy on her arm and we didn't. Only this time she didn't have a boy – she had this old married guy and she wasn't even getting any out of it. But that didn't stop her from acting shitty towards us, and she got really serious all of a sudden, like, she started talking more serious and stuff, and it was always about ideas and things like that, and she'd say it in a whisper so the other kids didn't think she was a tool or something. It was like she was slowly becoming an adult from hanging around the guy.

But she still, like, talked to me, and I wanted her to because I was, like, really curious by this point. You know? She told me how Sung would cook these bizzaro Korean meals, like fish with their heads still on and some spicy red cabbage thing, and spiced up cucumbers that were like pickles but not pickles, and weird Korean noodles that were soft and springy like wire. Maddie said that Ted would always talk to her and listen to her problems with his chin propped on his hands and Sung would be in the kitchen, like, by herself, cooking, and that neither one would talk to Sung until she was done cooking and serving the food. She said Ted was really a good listener, which probably means that she was boring him to death. But anyway, she also said that after dinner they would watch the movie, or whatever, and Sung would go upstairs and go to sleep early and invite Maddie back the next night. Maddie said Sung didn't seem to be jealous or anything like that. I think Maddie really liked those times when Sung was out of the picture, so she could pretend to be in love with Ted, because that's the kind of person Maddie is. She lives in a freaking fantasy world.

It was really hard for Maddie though, because, I mean, she couldn't exactly tell her parents that she was going over to a grown man's house, even if it was innocent. She'd lie to them and say that she was going out with the girls, and then she'd drive her car down the block. I mean, I had to stop calling her parents because I never knew if I was supposed to be out with her or not. I guess her parents never noticed, since they worked all the time anyway. I also know she suspected that Sung hated her and would spit in her cabbage or give her a dirty glass. It's possible she was on to something. Once Maddie said she asked Ted if Sung was weirded-out at all by the fact that he was friends with her, but he said she wasn't, and he patted her on the shoulder and said that she could relax with him, and that he wanted his home to be a kind of second home for her, and that if she ever needed anything, she should, like, confide in him and let him take care of everything. I have to admit, I wanted a Ted for myself. I kept thinking, why should it happen to miss-goody-two-shoes? I was prettier than she was, and I have a more interesting personality and stuff, and a better body by far, and I'm a nicer person by far when it comes down to things like treating people nice and stuff, and talking to them. I'm a good listener and all that. It just didn't make any sense.

Then one day Maddie told me there was another woman in the house. Sung was there in the kitchen as usual, and there was another woman, Kylie, who was upstairs mending Ted's clothes and dusting. Maddie asked him right away about her, because she thought Kylie must be his maid or something, and that it probably wasn't a big deal at all. But I knew something was up. I knew Maddie had all kinds of wild suspicions, and maybe they weren't wrong. I just felt something wasn't right with this situation, and I had to find out the only way I could – in person.

Maddie

I realize I was trying to be more mature than the limitations of my age could possibly allow me to be, but I did want to foster the friendship. I did. I wanted to grow, and I still don't think there's anything wrong with that.

What ruined everything was that Amy insisted on knowing every detail, as if it was so exotic for a young woman to be friends with an older man, as if it had to be tagged like some rare animal. She just wouldn't leave me alone. "I'm curious," she would say. "I just want to know." This was twenty-four seven.

But as much as I wanted to, I could never deny Amy her gossip. I suppose it was my own weakness. In retrospect, I guess what I really wanted to tell her was that I didn't think we had anything in common anymore, that our interests were too varied for us to really maintain a productive and growing friendship. She was just a jealous little girl, who constantly tried to act like she knew me better than she actually did. But she wasn't interested in challenging herself, or growing anymore. I honestly just didn't have much use for her anymore.

Then it turned ugly. Amy started saying vicious and completely

– let me emphasize that – completely untrue things about Ted and me. She called me up one day, asking about details. I just woke up from a nap and I was tired and cranky, and I didn't feel like replaying my whole life for her. I wasn't using my full judgment, but when she asked: "So, has Ted ever slipped you any uppers from the old folks home?" I snapped.

"What kind of relationship do you think I have with him, Amy?"

Amy mumbled and grumbled and tried to evade the confrontation, but that time I didn't let her off. I wanted to know what she really thought.

"I don't know. I've never met the guy."

"That's right," I said. "You haven't." She cleared her throat in a half-laugh, as if I was making a big deal out of nothing.

"Well, when can I meet the guy then?"

"Why does it matter to you so much? He's only my neighbor."

"I'm so glad," she said with a fake choking cry. "I'm glad you think so highly of me, Maddie." I gave in. Fine, I told her she could meet him some day, and that he'd be happy to meet someone like her. But really I just said it to be nice. I didn't actually expect her to take me up on it.

Wouldn't you know it, the next night she showed up at my house. I was doing my physics homework when I heard a ring at the door. My parents were both at work, so I answered the door, and there she was. She was dressed in this low cut red blouse, and lots of thick, skanky makeup, and a black leather mini-skirt that I never saw before. I mean, I could smell her sweet, flowery perfume through the storm window.

"Jesus, Amy. Why are you dressed–"

"I was just, like, in the area," she said. "I thought I'd say hi."

"Amy, we live in the same area," I said. "You're always 'just in the area.' You came because–" But she cut me off again. She didn't want me to acknowledge the obvious. Instead she let herself in, and asked me what I was doing, and I told her. She asked if she could do homework with me.

"Well, I'm supposed to go to Ted's later. Sung is making this special soup dish, and they want me to join them. It's a very special occasion."

"Actually, this might be a good time to meet them," she said. "Don't you think? I mean, I'm right here, aren't I?"

I told her that it really wasn't appropriate to invite her over at the last minute, and that it would be fine with me if she came another time, but that I didn't want to impose upon Ted and Sung, especially since they were kind enough to feed me. Well, Amy went ballistic. "You know, you're not holding up your end of our friendship," she said. She said that I had to let her meet Ted because I'm her close friend, and she wanted to meet my friends, and that she had the right to do whatever she wanted, and that she might just drop in anyway. She said I "promised" to introduce them. But I never promise anything.

In retrospect, I should have just been rude and called Ted and told him that I would like to have Amy over briefly to meet them after dinner. He would have been agreeable to that; in fact he would have been agreeable to the idea of me dropping by at any point in time. But Amy's insistence grated on my every nerve, and I tensed up and just didn't want to do anything she said. I was suddenly ready to do anything I could to stop her from coming over.

"Well, you don't know where he lives," I said.

"*That's* not a problem," she said, and walked away from the house. Then I called Ted.

Ted

She called me up in a state of panic and told me, and I should say it didn't surprise me. I guess I'd think it was strange too if I was her girlfriend. She told me that this girl Amy had some sort of fixation with her, and that this girl couldn't get used to the idea of us. I told her Amy could come over if she wants, no problem at all here. The heck if I care. Sung was cooking up her me-shing soup and I was kicked back on the sofa with a beer. I was happy as a clam no matter what.

But Maddie sounded all torqued up, and usually she's pretty even, unusually even. She started asking all these questions about Kylie and my relationship to Kylie, and that's where I draw the line, see.

"Kylie?" I said. "Look, first things first. I'm not some sort of pervert or anything of the sort, if that's what you're trying to say now. Kylie is just my help. That's that."

Maddie kept on pressing, flailing.

"I don't feel that I have to answer these types of questions from you," I said. "If you're coming over for dinner, then come on over, but until then, I need to get back to nursing my beer."

Here's what happened next. She came over. We ate the dinner and Sung was in the kitchen doing the dishes. The dishwater was slopping in the sink, and she had her country station on in the background. Maddie said she needed to talk to me before Amy came over.

"I think we've become good friends," she said, "and I want to continue. But it's hard. Nobody seems to understand, that...you know. You know..."

"What? That I'm not–"

"Yeah, that you're not fucking me, or something," she said. Her arms were crossed at her stomach, and she was rocking back and forth on her knees, making her look like she had a stomach ache. "Have you thought about it?"

"What?" I said dumbly. I didn't want to proceed down that path, but there she was confronting me about these things. It was entirely uncalled for. After a bit of stumbling and stammering, I was out with it.

"Of course I've thought about it. How could any man not think about it? But the point is that's not how I usually think about you, see?"

There was this moment where she just rocked and rocked, with no regard for me, or where she was, as if she was summoning ancestral spirits right there in my living room. Then she stopped, and she stood up over where I sat, and she said, "That's a very honest thing to say," and she plopped down right next to me and put her arm over my shoulder. Then, without irony she said, "Honesty is important to me, you know."

Well, this just blew my mind, so I decided to go whole hog and tell her all my feelings on the subject. It seemed like I could when she was sitting there with her arm around me in a full buddy-buddy position.

"Here's the deal," I said. "As far as Kylie is concerned, I have to admit, I hired her because she's young and untainted. She's only seventeen, if you'll believe that. I want to be friends with you because you're a kindred spirit of a sort, and you're young and unspoiled too."

"That's it?"

"Maddie, if you want to know the truth, I have a problem with, you know, women in general."

"What's your problem?"

"My problem is I hate them. Okay, there. I said it."

At this Maddie shot out an uproarious drunken laugh, although she hadn't had a sip of anything. Nervous.

"Then why did you marry one?" she asked.

Then I had to tell her the whole boring story about how we met when I was teaching in Korea for a year, and how it was an arranged marriage of a sort. I told her how I taught Sung's sister Huyang, and her father was so happy at their daughter's progress they offered me the opportunity to date Sung, and that Sung ended up liking me enough, and after a few months we were hitched. Blah, blah, blah.

"It wasn't exactly a whirlwind romance, but it was quick," I said. "Most Korean women are so passive they would foot-bind themselves if they could. Sung," I whispered. "Sung isn't filled with all that American entitlement."

"So maybe what you don't like is American women," she said.

"All women are becoming American women," I said. "What do you think McDonald's is about?"

"Well, I can see your point," she said. "What makes me better though? I'll be a woman, right? Is there a time limit to me? Is that what you're saying?"

I thought long and hard before I answered that one. I listened to Sung drying the pots and pans in the kitchen, and the skwaaak sound of the drain undraining, and I knew I didn't have much time.

"You look at little girls today and they're learning all these techniques to break down male defenses. They learn the eye-bat, they learn the pout, they learn the cry. These girls learn that all you have to do is pull on the right strings and a man will be yours. That's why I hate women. They have all these abilities, and they just try to manipulate me. It pisses me off. They make me feel guilty for just existing."

Then I told her all about Sung's problems, how she had to get a prolactin test that week to confirm or deny the brain tumor. I wanted to make sure Maddie knew I'm not a monster, and that I do care about Sung. I told her I don't hate Sung, and I don't hate most women, but as a group sometimes...well, sometimes they wear on my every last nerve. Girls are different though.

As far as the time limit, I didn't say anything because at that moment there was a knock at the door and Sung entered the room, and I had to turn my attention elsewhere.

Amy

So I got there and they all, like, stood there watching me, like I'm this big freak of nature in the doorway, trying to, like, prove something. I got this big whiff of fish smell, and celery or something, and I was surprised. I never expected to see Maddie in this kind of environment, and there she was surrounded by two strangers who were staring at me like *I* was the stranger, even though I'd known Maddie for like a thousand times as long as they had.

"Hi," I said. "I'm Maddie's friend. I'm Amy."

They greeted me warmly and Sung offered me a Coca-Cola and some candy, but I said I just wanted water. Ted told me he wanted to give me the tour, and he took me all over the house, into the bedrooms, bathrooms, and kitchen, even the garage. I felt right away that he was trying to prove to me that nothing was going on. He wanted to show me everything so that I thought there was nothing to hide. At one point I almost turned to him and said, "You don't have to try so hard; you're not doing anything wrong." But the whole thing just creeped me out. It wasn't their house, which was, like, completely regular. Ted seemed like the nicest guy in the world, and Maddie seemed comfortable. Which is, I guess, what I didn't like.

See, here's the thing: I had to do this report on Franciscan monks once. I read about all these guys and how they lived in these isolated areas, with like nobody around. And they didn't speak to each other, and they prayed all day. I had nightmares after that. I just, like, couldn't see how anybody could live their lives all separated and away from people. It's like they didn't care what anybody thought about anything, and they didn't care what was going on in the world or anything outside of what they were doing. This whole thing with Ted and Maddie was on the same level: it just, like, weirded me out that they didn't go by what most other people did in life.

So they sat down to dinner, and Sung offered me some of the Korean food, and I didn't eat any of it cause it, like, all smelled like nasty fish stink if you ask me. But they were all very nice to me. Sung wanted to get me fresh Coca-Cola every two minutes, and Ted asked if I wanted to hear any music on the stereo, even if all he had was, like, old seventies folk music. They asked me questions about how school was going, and things about my family – friendly stuff like that. Maddie wasn't too bitchy either. She just sat there eating her dinner, and drinking her water. Just regular stuff.

Afterwards I helped clean up and then I said I needed to go home and study for a test, even though I didn't. So I thanked them for the opportunity to meet them, and I drove home. When I got in the door, my mother asked where I was and I told her I was just visiting Maddie, and my mother wanted to find out how everything was going with her, but I just didn't feel like talking about it unless I could bend it. Instead I called Officer Gorman. I told him what I told him before about Ted and Maddie. But this time I gave him names, addresses, phone numbers. I, like, gave him everything he wanted. "Have you ever met these people? Could you identify this guy?" he asked me. "Yes, sir," I said. "But don't make me confront him. I'm afraid to see him." And then I went to sleep, and I didn't dream a thing.

Eggs

I'll start with the display. Right, my father's display. He kept his in a room on the new wing. He built the wing, designed it especially for them. The room was about the size of this one, but just eggs. Nothing else. Cases and cases of those gorgeous eggs. Right. Behind locked glass. He had his duplicate eggs in airtight cases in a storage complex, right down the road from here actually. Those? The prize eggs, the ones nobody but me saw, were kept in a safe under a panel under the master bed. The combination to that thing had seven digits, and I was the only one he trusted with it. Are you really?

Well, I'll tell you. As you walked into the room on the right, he had three cases of emu and ostrich eggs. One or two rhea. I forget. I forget. Yeah, of course decorated. Until later he didn't collect anything but the best decorated eggs. But those big ostrich eggs aren't froufrou – you could just about stand on an egg and not break it. Since I'm two twenty plus – and don't even ask if I'm pregnant – there's no way I could, but that's a different issue altogether. So he started collecting these ostrich eggs first – trip to Kenya – so they got the first logical position in the room. A lot of those artists are world famous. Faraji Kito. Xola Kanelo. Kwesi Adofo. Hamidi Ubani. All the big boys.

In the first case alone he had a Sule Diara depicting a Japanese garden. The nobleman, with his fu-manchu look and ocean-colored gown holds a fan and leers at a noblewoman who bends towards him from a lily pad with a come-hither expression. At the bottom of the egg a bouquet of lilies, asters, roses in front. Beautiful lily pad stand in gold. Right next to that you have an emu egg decorated with a sash of gold and inlaid pearls, with a pearl crown capped with a fleur-de-lis. Yeah, from some French-speaking African country or another. Gold tassel lightly grazing the gold stand. Oh, thousands. I mean. Hundreds of thousands for some of them. Right next to that one my father kept a jewelry box egg. It was this gold-plated egg with rhinestones in the shapes of roses. The inside of the box was lined with a velvet interior and depicted the coronation of a prince with surrounding knights, and various nobles. A wide stripe of gold and rhinestones separated the two halves, and the whole thing was capped with a dome of rhinestones. And so on. I could describe those eggs all day long.

 Hold on. It's Cutex. No, it was Pam yesterday. Usually alternate. Cutex. Pam. Cutex. Pam. Oooooohhhhhhhhhhhhhhhhhhhhhhhh. Heeeeeeeeeee eeeeeeeeeeeeeeeeeeeeeeeeeeeeeeeeeeeeeeeeeee. Yes. When he wasn't around, back then, I'd do some potpourri spray, some Pam, some gasoline or butane fuel, and I'd unlock that room and just walk around with my sniff and my paper bag, you know. Admiring the beauty of those things. Yeah, I've done that. Yeah, that too. No, I'm twenty-three. Graduated last May. Was it May? No the May before that May. I think that was the May. I forget. I figured I'll just come home and hang out with Pops. People call me lazy, but the way I see it, we live in the richest country in the world. I feel inclined to take full advantage of that. You didn't hear people in 17th century France calling each other lazy for just sitting on their asses and talking about ideas in those salons and what not. Especially if you were a woman. They knew what they wanted to do. That's the kind of life I want to lead: an existence of absolute disgusting leisure.

 Hold on. The high only lasts for a minute, then I'm back to normal. It depends. It intensifies. Don't worry about that. It's just blisters and a rash. I just put some Chapstick on it, you know? Ointment and shit like that. Headaches sometimes. Cough sometimes. Not bad, all things considering. This? This is from my boyfriend. Jack.

 So you want some back-history, or you want to sit here and talk about my blemishes? Okay. Well, as you know, he used to be a big time broker. He was raking in three or four mil a year. I mean, my father was one of the top fifty brokers up there. Yeah, we lived down here. He flew up on Sunday evening, and would come back down on Saturday, then turn right back around the next day and do it all over. When you're making fifty thousand a week, who cares about airfare? He did that for ten years, then retired, you know? Bought the house.

RANTS AND RAVES

Got into those eggs from that old Forbes guy, you know. The older one. You didn't know that? That man has the world's largest collection of Fabergé eggs outside of Russia. Showed a couple to my father, and that was all she wrote. That's when he went to Kenya. Went on a safari, but also heard about all the places you could get cheap quality eggs. Came back with two boxes filled with them, including the ones I just told you about. He just fell in love with the things.

What? Well, I thought it was healthy. I thought it was good. I mean, with Mom in Oregon with my stepfather, and my sister out there too, he needed something to keep himself steady. I wanted him to have a pastime. What did I care? But I didn't know it would get this insane. Because he was never there. I mean, never. One day a week. Not even twenty-four hours sometimes. She went crazy. She couldn't handle that. I don't blame her at all. Nope.

He was insatiable. He owned at least one by every quality artist in the world. His emu and ostrich collection alone is worth some people's houses. Then he got into the high-class eggs, the Fabergé-style shit. You know? No, he never cared about crystal eggs or carved mahogany. And none of that Fenton crap. No unicorns, or rainbows, or Jesus and cherubs floating in the sun-glossed sky. That's flea market dreck. I'm talking about real eggs. He doesn't want the *form* of an egg. My theory? He wants to take pleasure in the fact that here's the product of a woman animal that went unfulfilled. It was innocent enough with the emu and ostrich eggs, but when my father started in on the Fabergé style, that's when all hell broke loose. He started studying them all day long, just hiding out in that room and looking at his eggs.

No, I mean he wasn't insane. He'd catalogue them and organize them, but he was obsessed with those eggs. My father never did anything half-assed. That's why my mother left him. Before it was stocks. Then it was eggs.

Then my father started developing rivalries. A man with a mission. My father would always tell me, "You're the only woman that I'm even going to let near my collection." Once he woke me up at 4:30 in the morning, right? He said, "I've decided something." I rubbed my eyes and tried to focus on what was happening. "I'm going to wipe all those fucking bitches out of this hobby! That's just the way it's going to be. You got that. I'm going to destroy those women!" I mumbled something and fell directly asleep. Subconsciously I just tried to shut it out.

    That's what I'm getting to. He started with a woman named Carla Dinkins. Yeah, put that in your notebook. Mr. Editor will eat this up. No, she lives over in Kent County. Half an hour away. My father found out about Carla when he went to one of those egg shows. It's like any other kind of collectible show. People set up tables of their collectibles and try to sell them. Simple as that. Now, most of the men who collect eggs are just that – men. Not a whole lot of women in the business. That's part of the reason. Seems like most of these sort of hobbies are developed and ruled by men, especially the egg trade. I'm a woman. You're a woman. We know. There's that part of a woman that doesn't like the idea of killing baby birds to have some fancy decoration that you can put in a safe, right? Not Carla. She was one of the big shots, and my father took an exceptional disliking to her right off the bat. Thought it was unnatural or some shit.

    The night of that show up in Hanover my father came home with a bee under his bonnet like you wouldn't believe. He stared out into space and crinkled his nose, and just talked. He wasn't talking to me, but he didn't care that I heard. He was just expressing himself. "That woman had some nerve even being there. Didn't she know she wasn't wanted? Doesn't she know that we want a place where there aren't any of them around? Throw women in the mix, and everything is shot." He stayed up until three in the morning talking to himself and calling his friends in the egg business. I listed to him for a while. He was trying to convince his fellow collectors to insist on banning all women from future shows or seminars, but by his stiff posture and the tight way he swallowed, he was talking to deaf ears. At one point I picked up the phone. Yes, it seemed that crucial. He was trying to tell some man – Terry Wilson, I think – that women are the ruin to this hobby. "They are the ones that bring all that Fenton shit into shows, try to make a mockery of this hobby with their sentimentalized version of things. Women always try to *lighten* everything. To me decorative eggs are light enough. The time is ripe

for visionaries, not these two-bit mawkish women."
"But Bruce," Terry said. "There's nothing wrong with Carla's collection. She's got a fine collection. She's got some real nice pieces, you know. I don't under–"
"Yes, she does," my father said. "Yes, she does. That's not the point. It's the gesture. The way you set things out in life. Carla may be the exception – and believe me I don't have anything personal against Carla – but if we let her in, we have to let in any namby-pamby cheerleader out there." I could hear Terry strain with discomfort, and for a moment I thought he might hang up.
"Bruce, this is a free market," he said. "What you're talking about is nonsense. You can't enforce that kind of thing."
"It's not about can't or can, it's about will. It's about market control," he said.
Right, my father was in a fury. He couldn't be rationalized with. "I'm a visionary Terry. You can't tell me what can be done or what can't be done." That's when I hung up. I'd heard that speech a thousand times, and I didn't need to hear it one more.
Hold on.
Ummmmmmmmmmmm. Ummmmmmmmmmmmmmmmm.
Yes. Sorry. So. Sooooooooo. Ohhhhhhhhh. The next day I woke up to find two boys in the kitchen. One's almost fat as me, with long hair and four days of facial fuzz. The other one is skinny and short, but with an evil little grin. Spiky rat hair. Zits everywhere, even on his hands. Mean as hell. I don't know. They were probably sixteen or seventeen. They were sitting at the kitchen table with six or seven cartons of regular chicken eggs stacked next to them. I greeted them and asked them where my father was. Just then he came in with a needle.
"Good morning Vicki," he said. I nodded.
"What's going on now?"
"Oh," he said. "I'm showing these boys how you drain an egg without popping the shell. You know, the normal. These boys are going to help me out."
My father held an egg over the newspaper, poking the pin in the bottom. Slowly the yoke and egg whites dribbled down onto the newspaper. These punk kids watched it, smirking at each other. One

of these looks, like "What the fuck is this old man trying to prove?" I'd seen it a thousand times before, and went to get my Fruit Loops and orange juice. I sat in the next room. I'm not crazy about conversation first thing in the morning. When I was a kid, I used to stack cereal boxes around me to avoid talking.

I should have went back to the basics because it was just my father going on and on about how this is the way collectors get to the valuable part of the egg. "The valuable part of the egg isn't what's inside," he said. "That's just common protein, no matter what kind of egg you have. The valuable part is the shell. The calcium. It's like the reverse of what we're taught to believe. Forget about the soul. You know everyone says what we look like isn't as important as what is inside. It's the direct opposite of that idea in egg collecting. You have to reverse your thinking."

Yes. As soon as I take my first bite of cereal, you guessed it, I hear them talking about Carla. My father starts in on how she controls the market. "Imagine if you had to eat peanut butter and jelly for the rest of your lives. Would you go crazy? I would go crazy. That's what Carla is like. She controls the egg market." My father riles them all up, telling them how he has to intimidate her. Finally my father offers to pay the punks five hundred dollars a week each to help intimidate this woman out of the business. I doubt if those boys had ever said yes to anything so quickly in their lives. Then I understood what those chicken eggs were for.

Okay. No problem. Now when I say Fabergé-style eggs, I'm talking about the tippy-top of the line type eggs. Armand Hammer. Anastas Mikoyan. I'm telling you, they're not Fauxbergé. They're different. What I mean by Fabergé-style eggs are eggs that go all out to impress the viewer. Of course nobody has ever replicated the detail or precision of the original, but then most artists aren't commissioned by the Czar of Russia either. Fabergé's eggs are worth millions. If you look at even the least ambitious Fabergé eggs, you see a real attention to detail. Partially it's because he only made one egg per year, which he gave to Czarina Maria at Easter every year. But the money Fabergé earned with each commission afforded him the luxury of buying the choice of materials. You see silver, gold, copper, palladium, all kinds of gems and semi-precious stones like jasper, bowenite, lapis lazuli, nephrite. But my favorite part about the Fabergé eggs is the colors. He learned how to make something like 140 shades of enamel, which seems impossible, but it's true. His favorite was this oyster enamel that changes shades depending on the light.

Okay. There's so many, but probably the most famous would be his Coronation Egg. It's enameled a translucent yellow, and there are these golden starbursts all over, with these bands of wrought gold laurel. Black-enameled imperial eagles appear on each starburst, and on the chest of each eagle is a small diamond. But here's the best part: for this egg that was made to commemorate the Czar's coronation, not only did Fabergé replicate that inside the egg, he also replicated a miniature coronation coach with red lacquer. I mean all out. The upholstery of the original coach was recreated using red enamel. The glass was some kind of crystal. The gild coach was gold. Amazing. Amazing.

Anyway, the same day those punk kids came over, my father sat me down and told me he wanted me to start writing some speeches for him, and help him design brochures to sell some of his duplicate eggs. This was exactly the kind of responsibility I was waiting for. It wasn't as if I was doing much. I could help, I said. No problem. Then I asked him. I know I shouldn't have even broached the subject, since my father probably sensed that I was uncomfortable with it, but I had to find out about the kids.

"They are just going to help me consolidate," he said. "I'm getting to the point in my hobby where I just can't do it all anymore. I need their help. I also need your help." I left it with that and cleaned up my breakfast dishes. I don't know. I don't know why I didn't. I just, you know. That's all I really wanted, I suppose. I just wanted him to know that I was curious at least. I don't know what that means. How was I supposed to know that? No. No.

Anyway, that day I got down to business. My father said he was supposed to speak at a seminar in two weeks and he had to give a half-hour presentation on this Japanese rhea egg artist, Tanito Mushigawa. Since I have always liked a project, all lights were green. I don't know. I felt fine. No, I didn't feel complicit in anything. I felt just fine. I knew my father was in the process of protecting his interests. That's what people do, isn't it? I'm sorry. I'm getting defensive here. I'm the one that asked to speak to you, not the other way around. I've always supported my father. Part of me feels very wary about going against him in anything. Unlike my mother. Unlike my sister. They attacked him for all the reasons that you can imagine. Cause they're jealous.

Because I know my father is looking out for me. That's one reason. This is my version of tough love. He's lost touch with reality.

That said, I'm not just popping by for a cup of tea. I came here today for a purpose, and let me spell it out for you. The next morning, I was suddenly curious to see Carla's house. I knew my father had the boys tinker, and I wanted to see how much tinkering actually went on. So I snuck into his office when he was eating his breakfast, and I found the directions to her house in his front desk drawer. I ate a quick breakfast and then told my father that I had to do some errands, and that I would be back around lunch. He asked if I had finished the speech, and I told him he was more than welcome to look at what I wrote so far. "It's on my desk," I told him. As I was walking out the door, I realized my father was lonely. I knew that drove a lot of what he did. I don't know why. It's what you're supposed to do, right? Family's family.

I'm not trying to make excuses for him, lady. I'm trying to explain. That's the truth.

So Carla's house is down Route Nine. I mean way out in the sticks. I drove past pastures and woods and vast farms that dominate the land between the highway and the river. Finally I got there. I was right. Yeah. The house was splattered with eggs. The car was splattered with eggs. One window was broken. I wondered if Carla was still inside or if she sought refuge somewhere else. I wondered if the punks even broke into her house. I decided to knock on the door. No. I guess I didn't expect anyone to answer.

Well, she was tall and beautiful actually, with these long thin fingers. Her hair was cropped close to her head. She had an otherworldly feel to her. I watched her open the door briskly, seemingly unafraid of what might be on the other side. No. She didn't seem to be harried at all. In fact, the opposite.

"Oh," I said. "Oh. Oh."

RANTS AND RAVES

Hold on. Let me get another... Just let me get another. Cutexxxxxxxxxx. Ohhhhhhhhhhhhhhhhhhhhhhhhhhhhhhhhhhh. So. Oh. "Oh," I said. "I was wondering why why why is there egg all over your house."
"The Mongolian monkey dances on the table," she said. "Ohhhh." No. That's not what she said. She said that she had no idea. "The eggs just appeared. That's her life," she said. Eggs just appeared.
"Nobody broke into your house or anything, did they?"
"No," she said. "I was here. I'm fine. I'm fine. I'm fine. I'm fine."
"Oh," I said. "Well, I wanted to see if you were all right." Yes. It's true, that's what I wanted to do chickaboo. Boy. Cutex. Cutie-ex. Cutie-exxxxxxxxxxxxxxxxxxxxx. That might be a good idea. Water. Much. Thank you. Much. She was just a, a normal worm. A normal woman.

Yes, that's what I did next. I went back home. I was ready to confront him. Tell him off. Report him to the police. All of it. No. I didn't. Because he wasn't there. I got home, and he was gone. In fact, he didn't come back that night. I don't know. I don't know.

I sat right down. I had it all planned out. I was going to tell him how wrong I think it was to do that to Carla. I mean, there she is, a woman trying to make it in a man's world, and there he is, trying to squash this poor little woman down. For what? Why? I mean, I could sympathize. I can still sympathize. I hate all those fucking sorority girls with a passion. I hate the kind of women that made me feel inadequate and foolish, and all the pretty tarts in magazines, and the pretty boys they have on their arms. It makes me sick. But I don't egg people's houses. I'm quote comfortable with me. Unquote. I mean it.

Two hundred years ago, I would have been ideal. I would have been happier back then, when it was okay to love your body. Right. The reason it was strange was because I actually felt this moral upsurge. I just suddenly didn't see how playing and replaying some kind of resentment was going to solve anything. To use a journalistic metaphor, it didn't have any legs. It's just saying no. How many times can you say no? It doesn't make a yes, does it? No. No. No. No. Nyet.

Then he finally came home. I was asleep, but he pranced into my room. I could hear him. It was one of those moments when you knew what you should have done to prepare for the moment, but it is too late. I should have locked the door. He pranced into my room and leaned over me. I could feel him leaning over me and smiling down upon me like the sun. But I didn't stir. I didn't move. I knew something was wrong, but I didn't do anything. Finally, it must have been hours of him standing over me like a scarecrow. Finally I looked up, and there he was standing over me, this smile stretching across his face, from ear to ear, this huge Cheshire Cat smile. For a second I thought he might eat me or carve me into little pieces. It was that bad. Instead he patted me on the head. I could see his arm swoop down over my face, and then lift onto my head like some huge crane. He patted my head and told me I did a very nice job with that speech. He said he was very, very, very, very, very, very pleased with my work. Then he told me he wanted to sing a song to me. Guess? Guess? Come on, guess. Nope. Nope. Nope. "Humpty Dumpty." I swear to God's mother. To God's mother's mother's mother. "Humpty Dumpty had a great fall. Humpty Dumpty fell off the wall. Humpty Dumpty broke his eggshell. Humpty Dumpty went straight to hell." However it goes. I swear, I'm not making this shit up.

In the morning he was gone. I couldn't find him anywhere. I finally got a chance to confront my father about something and he was gone. I slept all that day. I would wake up and then go right back to sleep. I would fix myself something to eat and then hit the Pam. Go right back to sleep. I don't know why. Trauma? I don't know.

Finally, the next day he was there like nothing happened. I woke up in the morning and there he was sitting at the kitchen table eating his usual scrambled eggs with cream cheese. Just regular eggs. You never heard of this either. Well, he does. He eats them with a little cream cheese stirred in. It's good.

"Father," I said.

"Yes, daughter," he said. He was reading the paper, drinking his coffee. It seemed like a typical morning, but it wasn't.

"Father, what is going on in this house?"

"I'm eating my breakfast," he said. "That's what happens when you wake up before lunch."

"No," I said. I think I was wearing a towel or a sheet. I don't remember wearing clothes. Maybe I'm wrong about that. The hell I have. I remember everything just the way it happened. Don't tell me that.

"Why did you hire those punks, Dad?" I asked him.

"Those boys are doing a great job. They're going to be the best investment I've ever made," he said. "They just got me two nests of osprey eggs. That's what I've been doing with my time, missy. Like a good collector, I'm adding to my collection."

"Isn't that illegal?" I asked. That's when he jabbed me with his scrambled egg fork. Or tried to jab me with his scrambled egg fork. He swooshed at me, but I swayed out of the way in my towel or sheet. I forget which.

"Did you have them do anything else?"

"Yeah, they are trying to break down one of my enemies. Why do I have to tell you this? You know this."

"I guess you're right," I said. "What else have they stolen?"

"They will disable her," he said. "Then whatever else they have to do. Then move on. That's the way it's going to work around here."

So that was my father's next thing. The unadorned eggs. He had those two punks stealing every osprey, hawk, kite, and falcon egg they could get their hands on. Whisking them over to Germany, down to Brazil, over to African countries of all sorts. I'll tell you. He started with the National Zoo – hired some guy out in San Diego for a hit out there, up in the Bronx. Even zoos weren't safe. It would just be a quirky blurb to a journalist. You know the score, right? But to those birds, it was their heritage and legacy. This is when I started to get some morals. This was when I started really turning.

Right, everything sped up. Everything went really fast. I met a man. Jack. I was walking down the street of the neighborhood near by. Had to get out. I met this man who lived in the basement of some big house or another. He was my age. Worked as a counselor for retarded kids. I thought, what could be better for me right now? He approached me. Asked me if I knew of anything to do around the area. Yeah, he was new. I told him I could show him everything there was to see in about a day. Then I did. We were inseparable after that. Inseparable. It changed me. Softened me.

I don't know. Don't ask me that.

A week or two later, the punks came over for some secret rendezvous. By this point, I was fed up. A hobby's a hobby, but these guys were messing with life. They were careening into some international crime ring life, and my father was leading the shit. There was some big deal they wanted to pull off at Carla's in a few days. Break into her house. Steal her eggs. They found out she was leaving for a week. Well, I couldn't let this go down. No. No way. No, no, no.

I called her. I found her number. Ever hear of a phone book? I called her and told her what was happening. She thanked me, said she would hire somebody. That was the same night I left. Went over to Jack's. Then today, here I am. I'm telling you everything there is to tell. Then it's on to this lawyer guy if you blues can straighten everything out on your end. Unless... Anyway, I'm ready for a new start. Yeah, he's getting me something where he works. I think it's janitorial or something. Can't be that bad.

THE ABJECT

The spark: they were all unhappy. They wouldn't word it that way, but that's what they were. Their clarity was obscured by their intimacy with one another, and their blurry attempts to fuse crystallized emotion to unrealized cynicism. To them, "unhappiness" was something the abject felt sleeping on a park bench with a hollow stomach and a head filled with delusions – an utter extreme. Americans aren't unhappy, they thought. Americans just *are*. Yet when they exposed themselves to sharp inquiry, they realized they were, indeed, "unhappy."

Jason and Mark were best friends, and they spent nearly every weekend together. Jason's girlfriend, Helen, worked for a dot com. Mark's girlfriend, Trish, was a med student. They were journalists for the two competing newspapers. Jason and Mark met covering a high school bomb threat in Falls Church. It was six in the morning when they arrived at the school, both trying to catch a quote from the harried principal on the events of the day before. Both men had to pee, but the building was locked, and no port-o-potty in sight. Jason walked to the side of the school near the tennis courts. Mark did the same.

All things considered, Jason and Mark were both relatively handsome men. Jason was gangly, with thinning blond hair and a face like an almond. Mark was built like a linebacker, yet with a soothing, intelligent face. Crew cut. They were both dressed in khakis and brown sports coats. No ties. Jason had a quarter-sized yellow stain on his shirt pocket; Mark wore tennis shoes. The casual squalor of journalists. Peeing against the same wall, steam from their urine rose into the crisp fall air. Jason asked Mark if he used to cross-stream when he was younger. Mark stomped his feet. "I even tried it with my sister. But she was a bit of a tomboy." They plainly hit it off.

Helen and Trish liked each other in the casual non-descript way that friends can like each other without really knowing the other person, and the four new friends began spending time together every weekend   catch a movie, hike in the woods, dinner and drinks. Mark thought Helen was smart and gorgeous. Jason thought Trish was warm and funny. They joked about swapping, but not around the ladies. They just didn't think the ladies would have a sense of humor about those kinds of things. The ladies never said they wanted to get married, but Mark and Jason knew they did. The ladies never said they wanted to live with them, but they knew it was true. The ladies never said they wanted more commitment, but they knew they did more than anything. Helen told Jason, "Who needs pressure?" Trish told Mark, "What's the rush?" Justification. Consolation.

Jason and Mark started playing one-on-one basketball every week. They were evenly matched, and they played with a fierce intensity. After they played, Jason and Mark liked to get a drink at a bar down the street from the gym. The bar was small, with a faux-old-fashioned cursive sign out front: "Saloon." Inside, square and thinly varnished oak tables were precisely placed around the room. The exposed brick was undecorated and unpainted. They liked the sharp angles and the rigidity, though they would never admit it.

The men would talk about work, about their aspirations. The men would talk about the ladies.

Jason began confiding in Mark. He told Mark how Helen was obsessed with the prospect that he might leave her. He told Mark how Helen was terrified that she wasn't attractive to Jason anymore. He told Mark how Helen was convinced he had an affair with one of his colleagues. Mark listened without judging. He could tell Jason was discouraged by the relationship. Hoping to reveal some course of action that Jason might take, Mark asked him, "What do you think you can do about this?"

Jason told Mark that he had been with Helen for years, and that he had been faithful. He said he loved Helen, but that he didn't know if he wanted to marry her.

"She's the one that's been fooling around," Jason said. "She went to some conference last spring and called me on the phone – from fucking San Francisco no less – saying that she was soooooooooooo sorry, but that she slept with this man, that she fucked this man, and that she just wanted to tell me to be up-front about it. 'Honesty is the best policy.' Or so she said."

"So, what did you do?"

"I hung up. She called me five more times from California, but I didn't want to ease her guilt. I wouldn't talk to her. When she got back though, that's when we sure-as-hell talked."

Jason told him how he let Helen convince him it was a one-shot deal, that he let Helen coerce him into "healing with her," "growing with her," "becoming closer again." He told Mark that he felt like a sap, but that he didn't feel angry with her. No, it wasn't anger exactly. He told Mark that part of him was actually titillated at the prospect of another man screwing his girlfriend. "In a way, I'm proud of her," he said. Jason related the whole complex network of feelings he felt towards Helen, and that she felt towards him.

"I asked her to go to therapy," Jason said. "I just gave her an ultimatum."

"Has she gone?"

"No. She wants to go as a couple. But I feel healthy. I mean, if she walks out the door, I'll be fine. If she dies, I won't be crushed. I gave up on leaving her though. I'm throwing up my hands."

Mark in turn began confiding in Jason. Mark told him how Trish and he had been together for nine years. Mark told Jason how Trish and he broke up twice already, how they used to live together but decided it wasn't working, how they physically assaulted each other. He confessed that he broke a wine glass over her head once, that he could still feel a scar on the left side of her skull. He whipped her with his belt once in a fit of rage. Mark showed Jason the scar where Trish whacked him with a candleholder two years ago. Mark explained that part of this was rooted in the emasculation he felt simply being in her presence. "Soon Trish will make more money than me," he explained.

Mark told Jason of their religious differences, how she refused to convert to Catholicism, how he refused to convert to Episcopalianism. "You have to draw the line somewhere," he said. Mark told Jason about their sexual difficulties, how he only likes to bang her from behind, how she won't go down on him, how she begs him to go down on her. Mark told Jason about Trish's screwy family

– her neurotic mother and doting father.

"Part of me just wants to walk out the door and never see Trish again," Mark said.

"Why's that?"

"She's become, you know, such a part of me that I, um, I can barely divorce my personality from hers," Mark said. "If I leave her, I get a blank slate."

Jason could tell Mark was suffering. He tried to listen carefully, without offering suggestions. Jason could also tell Mark was holding back – that there was even more suffering to be had down the road. Mark's face was contorted in disappointment and rage.

"You know," Mark said. "I wish I was one of those men who could just go out and pick up women in bars and take them home and fuck their fucking cunt brains out. Or I wish I was gay. One or the other. Screw it. Heterosexual monogamy is for the birds."

"Literally," Jason said. "I think people get married to fulfill evolution. I don't mean just having babies. I mean, people are captured by what their bodies tell them they should be doing."

"Yeah," Mark said. That's why I'm not getting married."

This is how it went. The two men grew closer through their common distaste for their girlfriends. They could sit in the same room and talk for hours. They wouldn't think about food or what they wanted to drink, or eat, or that they had to pee. They were enraged and enraptured by their mutual fury.

In the beginning, Trish and Helen felt comfortable in their conversations, staying on the level of work and what's for dinner. They would have a girl's night out, but they wouldn't tap into their inner selves. They would eat at a Vietnamese restaurant, and go out for coffee, see a comedy at the multiplex, eat ice cream cones together on a park bench. They wouldn't mention Jason and Mark except in the most glowing terms.

"Oh, Jason's such a gentleman," Helen would say. "Why, just the other…"

"Mark's an honest man," Trish would say. "I need to be with an honest man. Without honest men, where would we…"

"He's so romantic," Helen would say. "You should see the

flowers he gives me, especially on just an ordinary..."
 Trish and Helen shuffled around the uncomfortable subject of their own contentment as if it were a flea-infested street urchin begging for nickels. Smiling and laughing, they huddled together in their silent and conspiratorial emotional bunker.
 When Jason and Mark were in their presence, Trish and Helen would act deferential and speak only in a reactionary manner. Helen nodded when Jason made a point. She laughed when Jason said something funny. Helen smiled at the right times, and clasped her hands together and tilted her head just so when someone had something serious to say. She knew all the gestures of common courtesy. She knew all the social graces.
 Trish would knead Mark's leg when he sat next to her at dinner. Her smile would be polite and cordial when Jason said something funny. Trish made witty remarks, but only after Mark's witty remarks. Then she'd smile at Mark as if they were in union together.
 After a year or so, Helen and Trish called a truce.
 "Look, Trish, let's face it," Helen said. "We're competing with each other. "I had to say it because I don't know... I feel bad."
 They were sitting together in Girard's, an icy California-cuisine restaurant. The overhead lighting was stark, almost medical. Hung on exposed concrete blocks were a green canvas, a yellow canvas, a red canvas, a blue canvas, a black canvas, a white canvas. The air ducts pumped the scent of jasmine and cedar over the tables. Helen was tall and robust, with a full Marilyn Monroe figure, small orange-wedge ears, and tawny freckles on her arms, neck, and face. Trish was short, lean, and boyish with a pixie haircut, and round beady glasses that she held in one hand when she talked.
 "I know, I know," Trish said. "I've been doing some reading, you know, and this one author that I really like – his name is Jorge Zygoss, really hot – he says that there is sisterly behavior and there is ex-girlfriend behavior. Sisterly behavior is when you don't try to impress all the time. You let your guard down."
 "Sure, I get it," Helen said. "I like that."
 They talked and talked that night. They talked more than they had ever talked before. They talked about how they let themselves be dominated. They talked about how they let themselves slip into

cruise control. They talked about how they did things for their boyfriends they wouldn't normally do for anybody else. Borderline S&M. Humiliating acts that made them hate themselves later.

"Why are men drawn to this, I don't know, degradation so much?" Trish mused.

"I couldn't tell you. It's like the big star with a cheap prostitute. You know. Getting away with something."

"Yeah," Trish said. "I don't understand that."

"For me," Helen said, prodding her peppercorn-flecked chicken Caesar salad, "I end up resenting myself, and then him because of something I let *myself* do. I don't want to disappoint him. It's really important to me to make him happy."

"It's this whole contorted maternal instinct," Trish said. "You want to take care of him. Your body tells you to nurse him. So you sacrifice yourself."

"Yeah, uh-uh. It's physical. I don't mean, physical-sexual. I mean, my body speaks to me – no, *through* me."

"I don't know," Trish said. She was eating her eggplant and spinach pizza with a knife and fork. "I just don't see the point of these people who say men and women work *because* of their different needs. They say that I need a man because it's the frustration and tension that make sex work."

"Well," Helen said. "I buy that on one level. Sex *is* more interesting that way. But what is sex? Sex is just one little part of my life. It's just a morsel. It's hardly worth mentioning."

"Yeah," Trish said. "It *is* overrated. I mean, they say don't marry for the sex, but then other people say it's the sexual tension that makes it titillating."

"I could be a nun," Helen said. "Uh-huh. Uh-huh." Trish licked her fingers clean, applauding the garlic olive oil and thyme.

"I was watching these two lesbians in the hospital last week. I mean, they looked so happy. They were so cute. They were sitting there in the waiting room, waiting for a friend or something, holding hands. One woman had her head on the other one's shoulder. I was jealous."

"Mmmmm," Helen said. "Sounds pleasant at least."

"Heterosexuality is going the way of the dinosaurs. Population-wise, I mean. If you sit down and think about it rationally, I mean, men and women are meant to be with other men and women. Men understand men. Women understand women. What's the big deal? It can't be helped. We have enough people already."

Their favorite bowling alley was what they called the "skuzz-hole." They liked the post-modern irony of slumming with the lowbrow white trash. This was the kind of bowling alley where the women had tattoos on their boobs, where everyone smoked, where everyone wore tank tops or greasy t-shirts, where every night somebody was kicked out for punching somebody else in the face. For them, it was like going to the zoo. It was "retro," and slightly dangerous. Jason and Mark liked seeing how they measured up the hotshots. Helen and Trish would never say so, but they liked being ogled by hordes of men. They felt hunted and animalistic. The men felt superior and sophisticated in comparison, and they could feel as if their girlfriends were worth ogling. It worked for everyone involved.

One winter night, on the way to the bowling alley, they passed a porn shop lit up in neon. Mark was driving, and pointed it out. "Hey, up and coming neighborhood, eh?" As they drove by, Helen poked Jason in the shoulder and said, "Hey, you boys can drop us off at the bowling alley and go have a blast by yourselves in the back." Mark kept driving, and turned the radio down, waiting to hear Jason's comeback. Jason just looked out the window and sighed.

"Oh, Jesus," Helen said. "Don't be so sensitive."

The four friends were walking toward their lane with their bowling shoes when Jason turned to Helen and said, "We're playing boys against girls tonight."

"Okay by me," she said, shrugging her shoulders. Mark and Trish went along.

As they sat down and put their bowling shoes on, Jason emphasized that the boys would pound the girls, that the girls were going to wish to hell they had dicks. He laughed, but he wasn't kidding. Trish said she was going to go find a bowling ball. Helen said she would go with her. As they were looking for bowling balls, Helen apologized for his behavior: "God, why doesn't he just calm down?"

"It's fine. No, he's just kidding around," Trish said.

Jason insisted that they play the best out of three, although the girls didn't want to play three whole games. Jason mocked Helen for using a nine-pound ball. When Mark bought Trish a beer, Jason wouldn't buy Helen one. When the boys won the first two games, Jason bragged and gloated, and pointed fingers. Helen and Trish laughed it off. They had fun anyway. They didn't care if they won or lost. Mark told Jason to settle down. When the four friends drove back, Jason wouldn't hold Helen's hand. He glowered and brooded and told Mark to drop him off at his place. He didn't want to spend the night at Helen's as planned. He didn't want to go out for a drink afterwards.

After playing basketball the next day, Jason and Mark went to their usual bar. Mark asked Jason why he flew off the handle at the bowling alley. Jason defended himself, saying that he didn't fly off the handle. Jason told Mark he didn't understand. Mark said he probably would understand if Jason would give him a chance. Jason said that porn was a touchy subject for some women. Mark told Jason he was acting like an asshole.

"Yeah, nice observation," Jason said. "See, Helen thinks men spend all day looking at porn, whacking off, and generally doing anything but think about their girlfriends. She's disgusted by the thought of men looking at other women's naked bodies – as if you have to seduce a magazine. She basically wants to control my thoughts, see."

"I didn't know," Mark said. "Look, I'm not criticizing you. I love you like a brother, and if you want to act like an asshole, you act like an asshole. I understand. I'm just describing."

"It's touchy," Jason said. "That's why I was so pissed off. We just had a talk. She ignored the 'progress' we had made and decided she was going to make the comment anyway. And she didn't apologize."

"This is ridiculous," Mark said. "She's the one that cheated on *you*. You let her back in, and now she holds it against you that porn shops exist? I don't understand this."

"I don't–"

"This is so far-out there," Mark said. "This is nuts."
"I want to be honest with my partner–"
"You want to just–"
"I want to be a man," Jason said. "I want to be honest, and she won't let me. It's not as if I spend all day thinking about fucking. Do you?"
"Of course not. Who does?"
"Maybe Helen does. She's the one that's obsessed with this shit. She wants to implant a V-chip in my brain. It's this woman-centered conspiracy."
"I can't believe this," Mark said. "I mean, Trish doesn't like it when I mention some actress that I think is hot, but if I had some porn mags, she wouldn't really care one way or another. I don't think."
"I don't know, to Helen and maybe most women, propriety and courtesy are more important than honesty. It's the ultimate narcissism. Helen wants nobody else to exist for her other than me. She is the only woman."
"You don't deserve this, man."
"I don't deserve this inquisition," Jason said.
"No," Mark said. "That's right."
After a few beers, Mark finally settled his friend. They changed the subject to lighter issues – football, movies, food. Mark told some stories, told some jokes, and generally made Jason feel better. Jason felt warm and loved by his friend. As they were walking out to the parking lot, Mark patted Jason gently on the shoulder.
"Jason, I have a proposal for you," Mark said. "You and I move in together as roommates. We see how it goes. We get rid of these cunt girlfriends, and go fuck whoever we want. No strings. We drink beer. We play hoops. We watch lots of Scorcese. And you know, if we feel like it, you know, we suck each other off. You know, we could both do worse. Just think about it. You don't have to have an answer now, just think about it."
Jason punched Mark in the shoulder, and nodded. "Sounds good, man," he said. "Sounds too good to be true."
"I just hope you realize," Mark said. "I mean this shit isn't going to just resolve itself. If we both get married to our girlfriends, we're

going to end up cheating on them, or resenting them or ourselves. I'm trying to just save us from divorce court."

"No, I hear you," Jason said. "I don't care for all the horse-shit effort. I'd rather get what I want when I want and come home to somebody who understands me. I'll seriously think about it."

Two months later Mark and Jason moved in together. They picked a two-bedroom overlooking the river. The apartment building was art deco, and inside the hardwood flooring was freshly waxed and seemed to glow. No more of this wall-to-wall carpeting bullshit. The faux-fireplace was decorated with an understated mantle with minimal molding. The kitchen had a gas stove.

"We want back-to-the-basics," Jason told the real estate agent.

Helen and Trish were shocked, and for weeks they did nothing but work and sleep. Then they began to huddle together at Macy's, feminist bookstores, go to lesbian bars for kicks. They wore flowered dresses and cardigans. Helen didn't want to see a man unless she had to. Trish made prank calls to Mark's phone number, until it was disconnected. Mark and Jason didn't give them the new phone number. Helen and Trish hugged each other and ate cheesecake. They rented movies together and drank wine. They hugged some more and listened to Schubert. They kissed and caressed and spent weekends in bed.

Mark and Jason told each other they were at the point of no return, and that they had to help remind each other that they each just dumped their respective girlfriends.

"We have to be strong," Mark said. "We still have dicks."

Life continued. Jason and Mark went to work, came home from work, cooked dinner, ate dinner, showered, brushed their teeth. They just happened to sleep in the same bed. They just happened to hold each other's naked bodies. They just happened to suck and lick each other's nipples. They would sleep wrapped in each other's arms.

Jason remembers that first night as pure bliss. They celebrated their decision to move in together with a bottle of wine, finishing the bottle in less than an hour. Drunk, they nudged and nuzzled each other tentatively at first, then more frantically, rubbing each other's cocks with their hands, licking each other's necks, scratching each other's asses. That weekend they stayed up late watching *Taxi Driver* and *Mean Streets*, drinking beer. They played basketball and talked about sports. They watched *Mean Streets* again. And then again.

Then they had difficulties. Jason said he wasn't sure if he was attracted to Mark. Even when Jason blew him, Mark took fifteen or twenty minutes to get hard. It felt good, he said, he just had to get beyond the psychological thing, or maybe it was the physical thing. He didn't know. After a week, they just held each other in bed. After two weeks, they slept on separate sides of the bed, ruffled each other's heads, hugged good-bye and hello. After three weeks, they shook hands.

One day after work Mark and Jason had a come-to-Jesus. Mark breezed in after work. Jason was already cooking an omelet and making a salad. Mark hugged Jason. Jason hugged Mark. The mushrooms, and onions, and bell peppers sizzled. Mark told Jason he thought about him all day. Mark told Jason he was worried about their relationship. Mark told Jason he was concerned that the fact that they really weren't "in love" would cripple them.

"I'm 'in love' with you, if that means that I do *love* you," Jason said. "But you're right. I don't feel gay. I have a hard time inspiring myself to get all hot and bothered, you know."

"I don't want you to hold that against me," Mark said.

"I don't hold it against you," Jason said. "I'm telling you we're both probably having the same problems."

Jason told Mark that he was glad he left Helen. Jason told Mark that he was glad Mark left Trish. Jason told Mark that he wasn't sure about the sexual aspect though, that he didn't feel inspired when he had Mark's dick in his mouth.

"I'm sure you feel that...blah," Jason said. "I mean, I'm not giving my all."

"I think my mind wants you to feel like a woman, but I'm having a hard time fooling myself," Mark said.

The two men sat at the table and talked about possibilities. The two men talked about returning to women, and just seeing how things went. The two men hoped that if they decided to return to women, it wouldn't hurt each other. They ate their omelet listening to Led Zeppelin, drinking ice water out of tall thin glasses. Mark complimented Jason on the salad. Jason thanked him. They stared at their empty plates as the CD ended.

At first, Helen and Trish were interested in all sorts of men. They decided they just couldn't be serious about each other. "We're not going to be dykes," Helen said. After their love hangover, they went to crowded bars in the city and stood around drinking White Russians and Fuzzy Navels, waiting for the men to line up. And they did. Helen and Trish danced with men who were older, men who were younger, men who were certainly richer than Mark and Jason. The first night, Helen went home with Kenneth, an environmental lawyer. Trish got four phone numbers. Helen told Trish she wasn't going to tie herself down, but Trish wasn't so sure. Helen never saw Kenneth again, but Trish started dating Henry, an economics professor at the local college.

Trish and Helen went back on the hunt, but Henry came along. Trish spent most of her time getting to know Henry. Helen danced with more men. Trish went home with Henry. Helen went home with Peter, a chef at a glitzy restaurant. Trish told Helen she thought Helen should find a man to date. Trish told Helen she thought Helen would be unhappier bouncing from man to man. Trish told Helen how sweet and placid Henry was compared to Mark.

"You have your ways; I have my ways," Helen said. "I thought you weren't going to stick to one guy."

"But I found a guy I like right away," Trish said. "I'm following my gut."

"And I'm following my gut," Helen said.

"If you say so," Trish said.

Helen started going out with other friends. Trish started calling Helen less and less. Helen stopped calling Trish altogether. Helen sent Trish a nasty e-mail, saying that she didn't appreciate her disapproving air, and that if she wanted to spend time with her, she'd start by trying to be a bit more understanding and a lot less judgmental. Trish e-mailed Helen a nasty e-mail, saying that Helen didn't like Henry and that Helen was more interested in finding rich superficial men and fucking them than in maintaining a friendship or a relationship. Helen e-mailed Trish a brief reply, saying that it would be better if Trish didn't try to contact her again. Trish e-mailed Helen a reply, saying that was fine with her.

A year later, Trish called Helen and Jason and Mark at work and said that she was getting married, and that despite their differences she'd like to invite the three of them over to meet Henry. Tea and scones. No presents. Face time. "Henry would understand me better if he could get a glimpse of my past," Trish said. They all said they would come. They all said they were happy for Trish. They all said they wanted to give Trish their warmest congratulations.

The day was cloudy and cold. Rain spittle glanced through the air. Wind batted against the shutters. Mark and Jason brought their girlfriends, Amanda and Rachel. Helen brought her boyfriend, Clark. Trish poured tea for everyone. Teacups clinked against saucers. Spoons stirred sugar cubes and milk. Mark slathered butter on his scone, and everyone else nibbled his or hers carefully.

"Good scones," Helen said. "What a treat. It's like merry old England. How quaint."

"Yes," Jason said. "It is a treat."

"Thank you," Trish said. "I'm so glad everyone could come."

"Me too," Helen said. "It's been way too long since everyone has gotten together."

Everyone was very cordial. Henry and Clark smiled politely at each other. Amanda ran her fingernail over the tablecloth. Trish and Helen stared into their teacups. They listened to the rain pick up and the wind clank the siding. Mark cleared his throat. Rachel sipped her tea.

"It's really nasty out, isn't it?" Jason said.

"Yes, it is nasty," Trish said.

"I don't like rain," Helen said.

"Miserable," Mark said.

They almost felt they were back where they started. But they never made it back quite that far.

ESCORT

January

Even when Marcel closes his eyes, the sooty clumps of snow remain – the windshields caked with rock salt, the streets layered with grit and sand. He never had to concentrate with such focus just on enduring. The banks of the placid Aniene, the view of Rome from the cliffs, the sere winds – even after ten years, Marcel was not prepared for winter. He used to dive into the cool waters of the river on Christmas; his brother would race him to the far bank; he would roil the silt riverbed with each thrust and kick. Every winter he's surprised, as if he half expected fall to skip directly to spring. Come January, West 51st feels like Dante's Ninth circle; Marcel bakes his apartment at 90 degrees, wears two winter coats and three pairs of pants. He'll sweat through the cold if he must. Manhattan will remain his Tivoli west, only more robust, crammed with opportunity.

Business is brisk, Marcel's clients readily ditching their New Years resolutions within the first three weeks. Yet, he understands the delight of internal revolt (that he can relate to these Janes is a selling point – they come to expect nothing less). Pablo's Bodega reaps the benefits as he stocks sodas, beer, wine, kiwi, mango, strawberries, coconut. He doesn't have time to buy new slacks, another pair of Vaasas. In December, he buys two gallons of Pasha, and by March, his supply is tapped.

Marcel wearies of the repetitive requests. Meet at the 21 Club with a dozen roses in hand; dinner at the Rainbow Room, and a Broadway play (Neil Simon, or the latest musical revival); hands clasped: "You are such a handsome man, you really are – I can see why you're so popular with us." He mouths the pre-requested, "You are a very beautiful woman," and "I want to spend my life with you and those luscious eyes of yours." There is the slow massage (standard coconut oil) to the sublime turmoil of Beethoven's sonatas; dangling mangos, chocolate strawberries and kiwi cubes over burnt sienna lipstick; slowly kneading thighs, breasts, shoulders, calves, labia, and standing to dim the lights to light the cinnamon-scented candle; cunnilingus in the flickering shadows as the CD whirs to a stop; slow but steady missionary position lovemaking, and the oh so gentle orgasm and final collapse. Many want to spend the night in between the satin sheets ("my hotel room is so lonely") – a request that Marcel immediately denies. "Yes," he wants to say, "if you can break away from your Nora Ephron-addled cortex, and/or if you have a penis tucked away in your Gucci purse, then sure you can spend the night. If not, you may leave the other half of the three fifty in the cigar box by the door. I will trust that you are honest enough to do that." Usually though, Marcel shakes his head mournfully, circles the pad, limp and routed, returns with the box and holds it, both palms outspread. A beggar. The Jane stares for a moment with a mixture of revulsion and pity (usually enough to send her on her way), steps into her silk dress, gathers her belongings, and drops nine crisp twenties in the box murmuring, "Keep the change." The last utterance runs parallel to a heavy glance of befuddlement and rejection, as if she expected to convert, cajole, or otherwise demonstrate and put into action a cocktail of pity, understanding, and benevolence.

This winter is no different. After ten years, Marcel has honed his shtick. He is well aware that unlike Johns, Janes want the usual, the expected, a dolled-up version of what they would want from their boyfriend or husband on their honeymoon or anniversary. Marcel is happy – more than happy – to cater to the odd request, but ninety-five percent are standard affairs. Marcel wonders if the social standing and lifestyle of these CEO's and lawyers coddles Janes to such a degree that their imagination is stunted, or if they are CEO's and lawyers because they never had an imagination to begin with. Marcel knows how lucky he is: he gets the chance to fuck well-healed women for a living. A decade ago, he's not even sure escorts had enough powerful sex-addled women to rub two sticks together. Yet he's weary, jaded, bored. Though Marcel's ennui hasn't spurred him onto a stint as a taxi-driver or copy-editor, he's ready for a change. This is not unusual, he thinks. Existence is wrought with adjustments, and one must self-correct to lowered expectations. You have to get used to disappointment, if not dismay. But when did sex become so banal?

February

Sleet and freezing rain. Colder. How is it possible? The Janes laugh at his long underwear and Russian-style coats, his Eskimo gloves and hat. He takes Mondays and Tuesdays off again, to catch his breath. He drags Theo to a leather bar in the Village. Ho-hum. Marcel always wonders whether he should take on gay clients, but decides against it once again. You shouldn't mix business with pleasure. Marcel asks Theo to join a threesome with another escort, but Theo declines. He feels taken for granted. He feels disillusioned, desperate. He tells Theo he wants a more adventurous relationship, something that will challenge him. Theo is pleasant enough, but too often represses desires, represses angst, shelves inner discord for later. It's been nine months. Maybe Theo will take it to the next level. Marcel decides to give him time, but offers a parting shot: "I want passion, Theo. I want things – us – to be very intense. That's me." Theo nods silently.

Chilled Midtown feels the fiscal doldrums. Broadway attendance is down, as is his in tandem. The day before Valentine's Marcel gets a call from a Mary Stuart – unusual to offer the name. She doesn't want just the regular, he deduces. She wants Marcel to actually meet her in the lobby of Le Parker Meridien, where she is staying for the weekend. He broaches the subject, a litmus test: most Janes will cringe at the suggestion, offer one of the bars. Marcel can hear the crackle of her smile. Mary asks him how she will know it's him, and he tells her about the Eskimo hat.

"A tux and that thing? You've got to be kidding. No, no, no. You come without the hat. The tux will be plenty. I'll be able to tell."

Marcel tries to relate his Italian peculiarities, but he sticks to business instead: one seventy-five up front, one seventy-five upon conclusion. She guffaws and snorts.

"Standard. You're going to earn your dough tomorrow, cowboy." Into the next day, Marcel ponders the voice of this woman, not husky, not throaty, not thin. She sounded sexy, he thinks, unique – but why? To Marcel, women usually don't sound sexy in the least.

They sound la-di-da, or uptight, or know-it-all. But this woman was the opposite: brash, demanding, insinuating, mystifying. A New Yorker? His bread and butter are silicon execs, Washington politicos, Boston advertising bigwigs. She's either higher up the food chain, or much lower. He can't tell. For a moment, Marcel actually feels desired. That phone call: in the back of his throat was the pungent aroma of the hunt. For once, Marcel doesn't feel the mere role of lover imposed upon him (thus the three fifty). *You're going to earn your dough.*

A long atrium with a painted mosaic ceiling and massive Doric columns leads Marcel into the lobby. A sheer cliff of flaxen wood backs the registration desk. Marcel has been here before. Yet, it is still startling. American capitalism at its most lavish, he thinks. As Marcel blinks in the absurd splendor, a woman approaches him from across the room. Marcel watches her walk itself, a study in affirmative movement. She steps long and lean, her calf muscles recoiling beneath her shear hose, thin black hair bobbing against her shoulders, arms swinging directly to Marcel. Diamond ring. Gold bracelet, thick as a pencil. Cardin watch. She's Chinese or Korean: Marcel fixes his gaze on her perfect brown thighs, the tan of her skin tone accentuated by the hose. She wears a blue dress the color of a late summer sky, a patch of North America. Mary slams on the brakes, a foot away, and smiles openly, warmly, curious yet sure of herself – scent of Burberry's, no it's Il Bacio. Her face glints in the light. Subtle, muscular shifts take place under the surface.

"Yes," Marcel says, mechanically sliding his arm through the crook of hers. They coast out the door without speaking, allowing the sophisticated hush of the hotel lobby to blend into street noise. Marcel carries his standard long white plastic bag, covered by another long white plastic bag. Roses. Mary carries a hand purse embroidered with rubies and garnet. As they step into the cool air, Marcel unsheathes the roses from their wrap, hands them to the lady with a gracious bow. Mary nods knowingly, well aware of the hackneyed gesture. She's done this before, he thinks. She must have heard about him from Enrique, maybe Vick. Her demeanor seems eager, yet all-knowing, confident but not self-deluding.

"Yes," she whispers. "Enough distractions. It's now time to fuck, you know."

Marcel nearly stops in his tracks. He asks her if she doesn't want to be wined and dined, the whole gamut. Is this it? Mary rolls her head and sighs.

"What is it with you people? The last thing I want is a romantic evening," she says. "My husband tries that crap all the time. Let's cut to the chase. Why do you think I called you?"

With harried excitement, Marcel whisks her to his apartment. Cab to the door. She walks out of her dress, tosses her shoes across the room. He cleaves the bra clasps, rends her panties, slings her against the wall. She wants it from behind. Silence, slap. She wants to be mutilated, castigated. Marcel is in love.

March

Mary flies up from Washington once a month– "meetings with the big boys." That's all she'll say. All that Marcel really knows is she's married with two kids. She says she's happy.

"Why can't I have a fuck on the road? Men do it all the time. I just don't want anybody. You have a reputation to uphold."

Initially, Marcel is fascinated by her animalness, a sense of mystery that he knows is clichéd, but still present nevertheless. She doesn't have to make an event out of the evening. She doesn't want to spend the night; she doesn't want to be his friend or confidante or shrink. Mary wants some central kernel.

They do talk though. Mary notices his bookshelf: Giacomo Leopardi, Giuseppe Ungaretti, Torquato Tasso, Michelangelo Buonarroti. She engages Marcel in conversation over whiskey shots (her treat– "this isn't a hotel"). Marcel is impressed by her analytic perception. She can pick apart a sestina, a villanelle. Most Americans couldn't give a shit about obscure two and three-hundred-year-old Mediterranean poetry. Mary speaks of Roman sculpture, Roman architecture, about Italian ham. Her recipe for veal scaloppine is heavy on the marsala, but it sounds close. She brings ingredients for risotto with clams, cooks a mean dinner. "Escorts deserve homecooked meals too," she says. Marcel is baffled: where did she get those littleneck clams?

Mary tells him she was adopted by a Mormon couple, and grew

up in Colorado. "Everybody should grow up on a farm," she says. She doesn't speak to them anymore, and doesn't know her real parents. "They wanted me to be Whitey White," she says. "Made me be a Mormon. Didn't take though. No can do." She couldn't track her real parents down in Korea. They may be in the North; she couldn't get a visa. They fuck, lie on the floor, and talk. No music. No pillows. No satin sheets. They listen to the sounds of the city, the heat circulating through the air ducts.

"Why are you an escort?"

"Who wouldn't like an easy living?"

"Is it easy? That's not what your face says."

"I get bored by the bossy WASPS and entitled princesses."

"Boyfriend?"

"Mmm-hmm. Can't stand my clients. Breeders. Snails."

"Huh?"

"Women. We bonded over this," he says.

"That's it? Money?"

"No. I have control over my cock. The more you are in this business, the less *thinking* you do with it. It becomes a tool."

"I wonder if we can't do something about that."

He tells her about his so-called rep: sensitive, romantic, Mediterranean. To his clients he's the sum of his parts. They don't *know* him; they know his type. He tries, tries, tries, not to just be a type. "They all want to go out dancing. 'You're a suave Italian stud. You must be a good dancer.' I hate dancing. I'll do it only if it looks like I might lose them."

"You make love to women for a living. You're supposed to cater to their whims," she says. "Isn't that just the way it is?"

"Unfortunately. I don't choose the company of women. Believe me."

"Me neither," she says, nudging. "Believe me."

She doesn't remind Marcel of anyone in particular. Her allure is deeper, bestial.

April

Marcel cuts Theo loose, questions whether he's gay at all. Maybe it was reactionary: sick of the clientele, the way hookers get. Theo wanted him to learn about politics and stocks; Marcel isn't interested. Marcel buys a grocery bag filled with Italian poetry. When passion peters out in one place, transfer it somewhere else. The last thing he wants is a relationship set in its ways.

Marcel reads Giosue Carducci to Mary, not as a romantic gesture, but simply to please her:

> *No more the hawker's shout and the sound of running wheels,*
> *No more the joyous song of love and youth arise.*
>
> *Raucously from the somber spire through the leaden air*
> *The hours moan, like sighs of a world removed from time.*
>
> *Wandering birds insistent knock on the glowing panes.*
> *My ghostly friends return, and gaze, and call to me.*
>
> *Soon, my dear ones, soon – be still, O dauntless heart–*
> *Down to the silence I come, in the shadow I will rest.*

Marcel cuts down on his client load. He knows he can't face bitchy blondes from Boston anymore. If anyone even mentions the Algonquin, they don't get a date. His escort friends don't understand, and offer him uppers, ecstasy, coke, but Marcel isn't interested. Mary brings her husband to the city– "cheap trip for him, plus a free place to stay" –though she still meets Marcel after the meeting. A good fuck and a shower. Then repeat.

"I feel at home here," she says. "You're breaking me in."

"I thought you were going to teach me the lessons." Soap lather. Shampoo lather. Hot jets of water against the back of his neck.

"It's not over yet, Marcel."

"True," he says.

Lesson number one: you'll want me to spend the night.

"I'm going to die before I'm forty," she says.

"How do you know?"

"Intuition," she says. "I just know. I've felt that way since I was a girl. I'd watch the goats and cows. *They* knew they didn't have forever."

Lesson number two: you will feel lonely.

"I became a Taoist in college. First it was all intellectual. I just wanted to try. Then it became visceral, and I didn't have a choice."

"Can you show me?"

"There is nothing to show. I just *am*. The way is within. Taoism says that you can't model nature. It says no first. This appealed to me. It's barely even there."

They drink whisky and water all night. They fuck and shower, and repeat. Existence is stripped to basic elements. She is blank, a bare wall, an empty sheet of paper, the receptacle for projections. Not on a pedestal, as much as the pedestal itself. Marcel is confused, lost, at odds with himself. She won't spend the night. She slaps him, short and to the point, warns him not to betray his principles.

"There is nothing unique about me," she says. "I'm just human. Just like you."

He thinks about offering May for free.

His client load picks up at Easter. They want to commit sacrilege, although they would never acknowledge this. They want to be profane, but safe. Mary reads his mind: she brings the baby lamb, and they celebrate their roasted abbacchio with two bottles of wine. The scent of rosemary and anchovy brings Marcel back – his mother would make it every year. With this adopted Korean, Marcel feels closer to his roots than with any of his Italian friends. He didn't even know he was out of touch until she opened the curtains upon it.

May

Where can we go from here? Marcel lies in bed pondering this strange turn. What can I do about her? She doesn't want me, yet isn't it human to desire her precisely for those reasons? Maybe this is why she's right. She's trying to provoke the human response, but she aspires to the animal instead. It's not easy being an animal; it's not easy emancipating desire, loosing it from human manacles.

Marcel loses his customer base. His regulars become frustrated by his moodiness, his restlessness; he's not willing to please anymore, not willing to cater to their needs. He allows himself to just be, but being doesn't make much dough. He takes long walks along the FDR Drive, the whoosh of cars soothing as much as the East

River. He looks out at the Queensboro Bridge, watching people actually moving, going somewhere, not accepting stasis. Sometimes Marcel walks down 59th and then all the way up 5th Avenue across 110th, and then down 8th and back around, making a perfect rectangle around the park, viewing the park from the outside – all of this is soothing. He buys boxes and boxes of Italian poetry, art history books, books on Taoism.

Mary doesn't know if she will be coming up in May. Her company is in transition, she says. "I try to be steady, but there are always these other forces." Shocked, Marcel finds himself weeping in the shower. He feels within her orbit. He dreams about a single flower surrounded by water. Every night the flower grows. Every night the flower is different – more petals, stem slightly thicker, different texture. When he wakes up, he can't remember what it looks like.

Marcel calls his only brother in Italy, who must be forty-two now. Marcel feels an urge to reconnect, drawn to the idea of returning, living with his brother and his brother's wife. He wants to discover what he came from again and leave the city for once and for all, start over.

Then Mary calls, saying she'll be up. She brings him a small blue vase. Marcel thanks her, and asks her why.

"Why do you think?"

"I don't know."

"I'm leaving," she says. "My company is merging with another company that's merging with another company. We'll be moving to California. So that's that."

Chaos. Furious fucking.

"You can't make up for it," she says. "It's not your fault."

"This isn't exactly easy to accept," Marcel says.

"I'm just a client."

Lesson number three: pleasure is fleeting. So much so it's difficult to tell if it was pleasure in the first place. He gives her a massage. Within the oil he can smell bay laurel, grapefruit, and lemongrass.

When she's in the bathroom, Marcel steals a business card from her purse. Writer. Journalist. 345 Connecticut Avenue.

June

Marcel packs his belongings. His brother sounds ecstatic that he's coming. His family will throw him a party that will last all night. They will make amatriciana with pancetta and buy the best red they can find, play music until the sun rises. Marcel feels united with Mary: they are departing separate, but at the same time.

His dreams magnify. The flower dominates the water. The flower must be cut. In his dream he must snip it or it will suck the lake dry. In his dreams he can't bring himself to do it.

He flies to Washington, takes a cab to the address on Connecticut Avenue. Marcel expected a mansion still, something to befit a woman who wears her clothes and jewelry, who meets with the "big boys." The house is small, wooded, set back from the busy street. He pays the cabbie and walks up the driveway. The house looks empty. The curtains are gone, and Marcel can see the empty walls from outside. There is also a car parked in the driveway.

Marcel's feet stutter on the asphalt. He wishes he could float to the house. He is more curious than determined. He knocks on the door and can hear movements from behind the door. A young girl answers the door, seven or eight. He asks the girl if her mother is there. She runs down the hall, disappears in the shadows. Mary appears, her steps stirring dust, echoing in the empty house.

"Mary," he says.

She looks at him blankly.

"Yes, can I help you?" The girl looks on from the end of the hall. She stands staring at him. "If you're inquiring about the house, it's already sold."

"No, that's not it," he says.

"Yes?"

"Mary, stop it."

"Sir, I'm sorry," she says. "Perhaps you have the wrong address."

"What are you talking–"

"Mister, I don't know you."

The door snaps in his face. He stumbles back to Connecticut, takes a cab to Dulles, a plane back to New York.

Then to Italy. His family welcomes him back into their midst, though his father is dead. His mother is dead, but he revels in the company of nieces, cousins, and nephews. His brother doesn't ask questions about Marcel's life in America, and they dance into the next morning. His family caresses his cheeks, welcomes him home. When he sleeps, he is able to cut the flower. He has the vase, and plenty of time.

Toothpick Jones
and the Hound's-Tongue Cave

A man called Toothpick Jones used to crawl on all fours into the caves of Clark County with his satchel and his harmonica lashed to his neck. In the satchel there was always enough food for the day, and a canteen of water, and a strong lantern that he'd light before he entered the mouth of the cave. Toothpick would crawl on all fours into the Hound's-Tongue Cave and spend the morning exploring the caverns, playing the harmonica as he walked and crawled along the limestone walls. In the afternoon he'd find a cavern he liked, and open his satchel, and eat his can of black-eyed peas with his fingers, and unwrap the washcloth holding his honey bread, and soak up the juice of the beans, listening to the sound of his own chewing in the dark. When he finished his food, he'd wash his meal down with the canteen water and dry his mouth with the washcloth. He'd pour some of the canteen water into the washcloth and wash his fingers and his face, and squeeze the excess water onto his dusty head, and fold the cloth into a square, and place it back into the satchel.

Then Toothpick would put out the lantern and play the harp in the pitch-black cavern. He'd listen to the sound in the cavern, focusing on how the echo bounced from wall to wall, from ceiling to floor, from floor to wall. Some caverns had a dull echo, and Toothpick would leave right away. Some caverns were too spacious and littered with nooks and crannies, and the cave snatched the sound away almost as soon as it left Toothpick's lips. But some caverns were so airy and the sound so pure that Toothpick would play the blues for hours, tears welling in his eyes from the sound of his own music. But this was one in twenty. Usually the caverns sounded like caverns.

The only rule Toothpick gave himself was never play the same cavern twice. It was a good thing for Toothpick then that Clark County had over two hundred limestone caverns, and when he played them all, he knew he could go to the next county over and play some more. But the Hound's-Tongue Cavern was the best in the area, and Toothpick was prepared to explore it for months if that's what it took.

One hot June morning, Toothpick was walking down the weedy trail to Hound's-Tongue Cavern when he heard footsteps in the brush to the left. He immediately stopped walking and peered into the thickets. For a while he didn't hear anything, but he knew somebody was back there from the heaviness of the footsteps. So he waited. Then he heard laughter and from the sound of it guessed it was two or three girls.

"Come on out now," he said. He wasn't about to put up with foolishness. For a few minutes he didn't hear anything, and he thought that maybe they'd head on out. But he kept waiting, coughing intentionally so they'd know he was right there. Then one by one three children crept from the brush, a tall girl with glasses, a shorter girl with a baseball cap, and a little red-haired boy.

"Sir, are you the guy that plays the harmonica?" the tall girl asked, her head staring at her feet.

Tracy, Mackenzie, and Kevin were off school for the summer with nothing else better to do than follow an old blues man around. The Henderson children lived with their parents, who were both park rangers at the national park, and who gave tours of the caves and the woods and mountains surrounding them. They loved the summers not just because they weren't in school, but because they could explore their own territory and live within their own imaginations. Their parents usually put their imaginations to practical use for them.

"I like to play the harmonica," Toothpick said with grave hesitation. He didn't want them to know who he was or care who he was, or know where he lived in the hills, alone.

"We like it. We like listening," Tracy said. She told Toothpick how they had been listening to him from outside the mouth of the cave. Tracy said the sound welled up from below as if it were emanating from the walls of the cave itself, or from the organ stalactites deep within the belly of the cave. Mackenzie told him that the Hound's-Tongue Cave was a wind cave, and that the sound carried out of the cave, and that other kids who lived nearby knew about the harmonica music but were too shy or polite or scared to say anything.

"Thanks for the compliment," Toothpick said, "but I don't want an audience." And with that he turned on his heels and made his way down the path leading to the mouth of the cave, but the children followed him and watched him as he entered the cavern. They sat near the mouth of the cave among the hairy weeds and purple flowers that gave the cave its name, and talked about their imaginary zoo filled with half-chimps and half-alligators, half-porcupines and half-cows, half-boas and half-eagles. Tracy was the first one to hear the harmonica, and then Kevin, and then the sound pulsed from within, and they leaned back to listen to their own personal concert.

Many years before, Toothpick was well known up and down the east coast, and he played gigs all over – even though he was married. He was married to a woman named Maggy Spritz on a boat floating down the Susquehanna with his friends and family there to pat him on the back and cheer him on in his new life. But Toothpick saw himself as a loner and a wanderer, and he knew he wasn't suited for marriage to a nag of a woman, even though he could be content with his life if he tried. A woman just wasn't what he wanted. She was perfectly nice in many ways; it was the role Maggy played in his life that he really didn't care for; it wasn't part of a musician's life to be tied to one place. At the same time he became bored with the same old standard blues tunes, and started experimenting, playing fifteen-minute or twenty-minute harmonica riffs, picking his steel guitar wildly until the customers fled for the doors. The club owners started saying he was trying to sound abrasive. Even though Toothpick Jones was once one of the most successful bluesmen around, when he strayed from the narrow path he was considered a lost cause. Business dried up.

Maggy encouraged Toothpick to rein in the songs and get back on the circuit, and for months they argued and then fought over what he should do. Although sometimes Toothpick agreed with her point of view, he decided to leave her before he hated her more than he already did, and he decided to set himself up on a Chicago street corner, playing the blues for pocket change, sleeping on Blind Boy Willie's floor and eating what he could. Toothpick had always been skinny and small-boned and fragile as the wind, but his street musician days made him even thinner, and he was slowly wasting away.

It was then that Blind Boy Willie told Toothpick of Chase Witherspoon's hut in the Kentucky hills and drove him out there with a box of food and a canteen, and he told Toothpick to straighten himself out and rest and get better. So Toothpick lived there with Chase for four years and then another year after Chase passed on, and he didn't hear from Maggy or Blind Boy or any of the cats from his glory days at all, and he didn't care if he ever did. He was content to play the blues on the porch of the cabin, and if he did hear from any of the people in his old life…well, he didn't know what he'd do.

So the Henderson kids listened to Toothpick's wailing harmonica riffs for weeks, but Toothpick would stay in the cave until it was dark, and he'd think or sleep, and the kids waited but could never catch a glimpse of him until the day on the path. Toothpick always knew he could have an audience whether he wanted one or not, and even if he didn't want one he got used to the idea of the kids around, and then he started liking the idea again. It was a new kind of audience for Toothpick. Toothpick never played for children before. Blues clubs were dark and boozy places, but here were these kids who maybe liked the bare sound of the harmonica as much as he did, who didn't need some highfalutin concept to explain it to them, and who didn't know or care who he was, and Toothpick felt it would be wrong to deny them music, even if he didn't really think of right or wrong.

So on the last day he planned on playing in the Hound's-Tongue Cave, Toothpick stopped in the middle of the weedy path and said "Come here, children, I have an announcement for you all." He waited a few minutes, and lo and behold, the children slipped through the bushes and stood before him in the sun. Tracy and Kevin wanted him to invite them into the cave, but Mackenzie was scared of the dark and didn't want to be trapped in a place they couldn't leave when they wanted. But Tracy and Kevin trusted Toothpick, and wanted him to trust them back, and Toothpick felt that and it made him want to play for them even more.

"I'll have a free concert today, kids. Tell your friends to come to the mouth of the cave around lunchtime, and they can hear me if they want. But they have to be twelve or younger or I'll stop playing."

The Henderson children ran back to their house and hopped on their bicycles and rode to every house in the area and told every kid they knew about the concert, and that they should come as quickly as possible. By the time Toothpick washed his hands and face in the dark, the Henderson children had gathered an audience of fifty kids. Then Toothpick played his harp as loud and passionate as he could, running through twenty-minute long versions of "Rambling on my Mind" and "Hell Hound on my Trail." The children laughed as he sung his rendition of "Milkcow's Calf Blues," and "Dead Shrimp Blues," and they clapped when he held a C note for two minutes solid, and they listened carefully to his blues version of "Happy Birthday," and they clapped when he finished, although they couldn't see him and didn't know who he was or what he was doing down in a cave.

Toothpick came out of the cave, and the children who didn't have to go home for supper greeted him as he blinked in the waning sunlight and flicked his lantern off. He bowed when they clapped together, and he told them that because they were such a good audience, he would play again the next day. Then he broke his own cavern rule and played the day after that, and the day after that for weeks until it was the middle of August and the leaves were drying, and the air became laden with dust and ragweed, and school descended upon the minds of the children like thunder.

One day, a woman approached Tracy in town. The woman was tall and beautiful with full milky eyes and a black dress to match her deep raven hair.

"I hear the children know a little something about a blues man around town," the woman said. Her voice was soft and calm, like the lulling whisper of a brook. "They call him Toothpick."

"So that's his name," Tracy said. "We never knew who he was, ma'am, but I know where he is."

The woman asked if Tracy could take her to the man, and she said she would, but that Toothpick wouldn't be happy, since she obviously was older than twelve. The woman smiled to herself, and Tracy wondered who she was and how she knew Toothpick anyway, and the woman wondered the same. To Tracy, Toothpick was part of the landscape, like the hills and the dirt and trees themselves and beyond knowing as a person or a figure of memory. To Tracy, Toothpick didn't have a before or after. To the woman, Toothpick was now just a dream from restless nights.

It was a Sunday, and the usual crowd of children was there, listening for the first notes from Toothpick as Tracy walked the woman down the path to the mouth of the cave with the church bells from town clanging in the distance. Maggy wasn't sure why she was there at all, except that she wanted to make peace with this man who had scalded her and brought her to realize she would never love again. Not that she didn't remarry Glendon King. She did. But Maggy knew that once you loved with every fire within you, any subsequent love would be thinned by the ashes of the first.

Maggy had called Blind Boy Willie and damned Toothpick to hell for the damage he wrought, and Blind Boy Willie shook his head and said, "It's a shame about Toothpick, it's a shame," but despite herself, Maggy found that she was curious, just curious as to what Toothpick had done with himself, and maybe that's why she was there. She wanted Blind Boy to give her the address of this cabin in the woods so that he might come with her and see to it that she was safe and satisfied with her reprisal. But Blind Boy wanted no piece of that, and he wished her luck and sent her on her way with a box of food and a jug of wine for the road.

As Tracy led her to the mouth of the cave, Maggy could hear the harmonica deep within the earth, as if it came from her own bowels, and she had to lean against an oak in the shade for stability. Tracy glanced at her to make sure the woman was okay, but Maggy was okay, just in shock. She sat in awe of what she witnessed, and Tracy watched over her until Toothpick stopped playing and emerged from within the cave.

Then Toothpick emerged blinking in the sunshine, and the children clapped, and he bowed his head in acknowledgement. Toothpick often wondered what the Hendersons' parents must think, but that day he saw the children and was bolstered by their support, and he felt content to his bones. They wanted him to play more, but he just bowed and thanked them, and felt content.

Then he saw Maggy. Toothpick never imagined he'd see the woman again, and was startled enough that at first he didn't know what to do. Maggy stared right through him, and Toothpick felt weak in the knees and leaned against the exterior of the cave for support. He just thought about his fear, and how a woman is the living embodiment of it, and it wasn't so much Maggy that he feared, but the concept of a woman like her dragging him down into herself and her maternal instincts, and her socialite sphere, and her feminine ways like a tar pit, and suffocating his every independent spirit. For some reason he was convinced that was the way women were, no matter what, and he felt nauseous and jittery at the thought of her presence, and his heart raced. The children watched him, watched the woman, and wondered who she was and why he looked so green and strange all of a sudden. Everyone watched to see what he'd do.

And then he was gone. The way the legend went, he moved so fast nobody knew exactly what happened. But the children who were there remembered: he slipped back into the cave. He moved so quickly he practically dove into it. The children gathered around the mouth of the cave to hear if he would play as he ran, but he didn't.

Of course there was some talk of following him down into the cave, but nobody had a light, and they decided to wait. The children waited for hours for him to come on back out, but he didn't, and the sun set, and eventually they all went home to eat. Maggy waited the longest, shoulders hunched in the dark until the moon rose and she felt herself slip into sleep, and then she too left, unsure of what to make of anything anymore.

And the fact of the matter is, to this day, nobody knows what happened to Toothpick except Toothpick. Some say he emerged from the cave once again, and hitchhiked across the country and wandered forever and ever playing that harp. Some say he got lost in the cave itself, and made it his coffin. Others say he lived down there in the cavern, becoming some kind of creature of the night. Others still say he walked right out of the cave, and back to his hut and never left the hut again, or that he moved to another hut in the hills and wandered on to new caverns in another county.

But that's not what happened. Toothpick scurried into the wind cave, and he took another passage to another entrance on the far side of the ridge. He got to know Hound's-Tongue Cave so well that he knew of four other entrances, and he chose the one furthest away from that Maggy. He didn't want to be chased, but shame washed over him as he walked through the caverns and emerged into the sunlight and walked down the path leading away from town.

Despite it all, he knew what he wanted to do. He knew then that he had learned something from those cave-playing years, even if he didn't know what it was, and that even if he didn't want to try again and find himself a woman to love for all the fear and loathing involved, he could see himself around children and raising them and teaching them to live a good life in the time that he had left. He hadn't a clue how this could be done, but he did know he didn't need a satchel or anything of the sort for that business. He shed the dead weight as he walked down the road into darkening sun. But Toothpick kept his harmonica in his back pocket, and he could feel the slight weight in his pocket as he walked, and that was enough.

The Ring

If you open your eyes, you'll see: soft bills passing between strangers, belt buckles unclasping, fingers burrowing in panty hose runs, hair twirling in between fingers, wedding rings unscrewing into pockets. Most people skate on the surface, accept the literal, buy into ploys. Drones. Career men. Ladies checking their lipstick in the rearview. However, the surface is useful if you can twist it to your advantage, if you can alter yourself without altering its perception – appearances.

I am getting married. My fiancée, Liz, is truly a "good person." She gives to the poor, adopts pets from the SPCA; she has a healthy network of friendships that she nurtures and maintains; she drives the speed limit, and always crosses the street when the sign flashes "walk"; she gives old clothes to Goodwill; she tries not to judge rashly, or raise her voice; and she never, ever says the words "I hate." I do sincerely love her – although not for the reasons she thinks. I love Liz not because she's a good person, but because she's an oddity. I literally had no idea that it was possible to abide by all of society's complex and unspoken rules. I had no idea it was possible to be "good."

Though I am in a strange sort of awe of her, I simultaneously fear her: Liz is the perfect science experiment, the ultimate government conspiracy, the perfect citizen. I love Liz because I truly do hope to attain her level of wisdom and nobility. Someday. For now I'll choose the opposite.

This is not to say I'm a Charles Manson. I maintain a decent (though dull) job at the Department of the Interior (my personal motto: "we do many interior things interiorly"). I have my own fair share of friends, and I try to abide by the law the way most people do – when it is convenient. But I have to admit, I have a terrible malicious streak. Every man has a beast inside him of some sort. This is mine.

My favorite day is April Fool's: I can get away with something that I'm not supposed to do. Last year I painted my colleague's golf trophy neon pink. At least I try. Yet, in my relationship with Liz, I've always been stable, supportive, and honest. I've never cheated, or strayed, and I don't think I ever will.

However, what has been rankling me of late is the incessant wedding planning itself.

I recognize this cliché of wedding planning complaints. Every man feels they are being forced to play doll and tea party at the same time. However, I've had it up to here with caterers, disk jockeys and bands, photographers, bakeries, rental halls, invitations, embroidered cloth napkins, spoons and forks and table cloths, tuxes and dresses, flowers and ribbons, slights and honors ad nauseum.

Of course, I don't share these frustrations with Liz. I sit quietly and smile in clean rooms, decorated with clean art, pillowed and curtained perfectly, heated or air-conditioned just so. We flip through catalogues that smell of rose petals and peppermint, and point to things we like or don't like. "Oh, that's nice," she'll say. "Oh, I like that," I'll declare. Liz pinches her skirt between her fingers, crosses her legs, crosses her arms and leans forward. She kisses me, and squeezes me, and says she loves me with all of her heart. I do the same and repeat what she says in a sort of pantomime. Everything is so perfect, and I do as I'm told. Even our parents get along. Her parents are nice and generous and supportive, and I suppose mine are the same. Silently, they shuffle pieces of paper to each other, like Mafiosos with envelopes of hundred-dollar bills. Marriage: perfect symmetry, a palace of an event. Everything and everyone just so.

When our parents leave, Liz cheerfully pours us each a glass of wine. I dislodge one of the pillows from the sofa, or twist the curtains slightly askew. I think of Persian rug-makers intentionally creating an imperfection in the weave so they don't mock Allah's divine precision. We clink glasses and sip our wine delicately. Liz purses her lips and creaks a pleasant smile, her teeth white and clean. We sigh and sit in silence, or sometimes play trance music (her favorite). Then I listen to the calming electronic drums, the digital rain, the sound of pygmies chanting. As a couple, we are top-notch at sitting together without saying a thing; Liz says this proves she feels "comfortable with me." Then she notices the dislodged pillow or askew curtain, and silently stands, and glides over to the imperfection, rights it and glides back to me, a phantom.

Recently I revel in my time alone, especially on the Metro. I just watch people, strangers, noticing the individuality of their faces and gestures, what they decide to read on the train, what they are wearing – as if the people on the train are individual shapes or numbers, as if they are small functions in a larger equation. These days, I price rings, trying to pick the perfect wedding ring (to me the engagement ring is just a starter). On the train I look at the wedding rings other women wear. Some are modest bands, but most sport unwieldy, thumb-sized diamonds crowning two bands – the fused engagement ring and wedding ring. I want to go all out, just like the husbands of these women. I want to be a showoff. I already purchased a one-carat engagement ring. Yet, I want something grander, more lavish for the actual ceremony. I want to upstage myself, blow her away. When I'm watching women, I can't help thinking, what do they really think about these things? Do they really care if they have a huge diamond? Are married women as materialistic as I think they are, or do they have a sense of irony about the function and symbolism of their jewelry?

When these thoughts flood my head, I open my briefcase, and pull out my sports magazine. Then I become one of the people I observe. I sink into a football, or basketball article and wait until the conductor announces my stop. Then I roll my magazine in my hand, pick up my briefcase, and step off the train towards the parking lot. I watch other men and women do the same thing. I like feeling as if I am part of a workforce, although I doubt if the workforce cares one way or another. I like feeling as if I am part of society, although I doubt if society would notice my absence.

However, I have impulses. I decide to interview women about their rings. I want to find out the truth about these symbols of marital union. I made money on stocks; I have savings; I have a Roth IRA; I have a 401(K). I decide to offer each interviewee one hundred dollars for fifteen minutes of tape-recorded conversation. Also, I will ask my subjects to interview them at their Metro stop, so I don't inconvenience them. Before I even begin, I am aroused by the whorish transaction, as close to prostitution as I am willing to go.

The first woman I ask is in a hurry and says no, and I wonder if I am fooling myself. Perhaps she thought I was making an advance on her. The next day I ask an elderly lady, wearing a purple fanny pack and a Cubs baseball cap-seemingly a tourist. Old people like to talk, I think. She agrees to talk to me, but says she won't accept any money (I thought this would lessen the allure, but it doesn't). We stop at Metro Center, and find a quiet corner on the second floor. I ask her about her wedding ring, and she says that her husband gave her the most beautiful ring in the world, not too big, not too small, not too garish. "My husband was the most considerate man I've ever met," she says. "I miss him dearly." I ask her if she ever envied the rings that her friends wore, and she looks at me funny and says, "Real ladies don't do that sort of thing."

The next day I interview a young woman who has been married for two years. She seems shy, and I have to yank answers from her. She says she never really thinks about her ring. "It's just sort of there," she says. "Like part of my body. I guess it's beautiful." She glances at it oddly. Her diamond is small, and the surrounding stones seem poorly cut to my eye. I ask her if her ring effectively symbolizes her marriage. "We're getting separated," she says. "If we get divorced, I guess I won't wear it anymore. I don't know. It will be weird just having part of me sit around a drawer."

The next day I interview a middle-aged woman who wears a power-suit and walks with an air of braggadocio. She will provide a good contrast to the others, I think. We stop at Galleryplace/Chinatown, and she offers to buy me a beer at a café down the street. I accept. She tells me I have nice features, good bone structure. I thank her politely. I drink three beers, and unclasp my belt buckle. I hope she is not offended, much less turned-on. Of course, the last thing in the world I would want to do is excite another woman on the cusp of my precious wedding. I wonder if she likes animalistic sex. I don't ask.

"My husband and I purchased our own rings," she tells me. "We both have enough income that we wanted to get what we wanted. We didn't want to be disappointed, or resentful in the least. So, I'm as happy as I can be about my ring." The diamond appears to be the size of a crab apple. "A lot of people are doing that now." She says the ring symbolizes what they can achieve together. "It's really a statement about our place in society," she says. "We are in the upper-tier – unapologetically so." She asks me why I am doing this, and I tell her. "Buy her something nice," she says. "Don't scrimp on the most important day in a woman's life." I ask her why a wedding is any more important than any other day. "It just is," she says. "I'm not a sociologist."

Today Liz is supposed to meet me at our Metro station. We have reservations at a new Malaysian restaurant. I get off the train and wait for her by the turnstiles. I like the sense of anticipation, watching the mass of random faces, and looking for Liz in the hodge-podge of people. Each face is different, each personality unique. A woman blows her nose. A man wears a straw hat. A short man slips his fingers through a hole in his girlfriend's hose. He wears a wedding band, and she doesn't. Then Liz emerges out of the mass, the personality and face that have come to love me. At that moment I do love her. Then my heart sinks – maybe it's just the love of familiarity.

Yet, the harried society in which we live is propped up by the slightest of supports. One hundred years ago, I would have worked in a factory. A hundred years before that, I would have dug ditches. Our society has lost its sense of context. So now I enter data and crunch numbers – what's the difference? It's no more honest or noble than digging ditches. I see these government bureaucrats wearing slick Armani-style suits, and I want to "accidentally" spill coffee on them, just to show them they don't live in the future. This isn't utopia. This isn't a dream.

I wonder if Liz and I shouldn't drop out of corporate society and become ditch diggers, live in a hovel dug out of a hillside without obligations and demands – a spare, albeit gritty existence. If she's such a good person, she should want to live a simple life with simple furnishings, and a ditch for a toilet. If Liz were such a good person, she wouldn't lead me into an ambush.

Instead, I decide to purposefully buy a forged wedding ring. I want some part – the supposedly most important part – of our ceremony to be to a sham. I want to acknowledge the fine line that keeps our reality from destruction. Moreover, I want to hedge my bets, but not by banging a stripper at some clammy bachelor party (a fleeting gesture). I want to have a seed of our own destruction already planted, so that if Liz leaves me after a year of marriage I can point to her ring and say, "Well, I always knew this wasn't going to work; even your ring is a fake." I want to know that part of my relationship with Liz is a fraud, to be reminded of the artificial nature of our marriage (and every marriage) every time I sit down with her to eat dinner, every time we are holding hands, every time we are driving on some romantic get-away. I want a reminder that things can go wrong, just in case they do.

However, actually purchasing a good forgery is more difficult than I expect. I spend hours hunting down a good paste-maker on the computer. Good thing I work for the government (seemingly I could be hatching assassination plans and nobody would seemingly know). I e-mail forgers all over the company, and after weeks the cream rises. A guy named Jakob Trollinger tells me he can make me the perfect fake diamond ring for eight hundred. Nobody will ever suspect, he says. He doesn't use synthetic GE diamonds, but zircon and clear quartz topped with a diamond coating. This way, he tells me, "If your wife tries the light test, or the bits of paper test, it should still pass. It will still cut glass."

Two months later, I receive his package in the mail at the PO box I set up for the circumstance. It's a thing of beauty, a three-stone diamond ring, Swiss cut, two carats, and all fake. I throw the packaging in the garbage, and slip the ring back into its jewelry box, then into my pocket. On the Metro I pay women to look at it. I feel like an exhibitionist. A woman in her exercise attire tells me it's the nicest ring she's seen in years. A woman in a brown sports jacket tells me she'd love to get a ring like that. A matriarch examines it and tells me my wife must be very lucky to have me. Throughout the ride home I maintain an erection.

I should have hired a wedding planner. There's the clergy, marriage license, lodging for out of town guests, receiving line, registry, videotaper, program, pew cards, blood tests, boutonnières, bridal album, presents for attendants, meadow bouquet or silk rose, plastic or engraved glass, bachelor dinner, pre-wedding party.

The wedding day comes and goes. Everything runs smooth as can be. Liz holds her hand over her mouth in amazement. She loves it. She eats the wedding ring with a fork. She wears it everywhere, shows it to her friends and family, cries in happiness. She dances with colleagues and drinks wine with her friends. I barely see her through the entire reception. Everyone hugs her, clasps her hands and tells her they are so happy for her. She twirls her hair in her fingers. Her friends ogle the ring as they kiss her cheeks and hug.

Then, six months later, our relationship is over. Over veal chops and artichoke hearts she tells me she's having an affair with a colleague, and she can't see breaking it off. She tells me she had to let me know. She just intuitively felt wrong about our marriage. I tell her about my fling with Rhonda during my trip to Houston. We decide to call the whole thing off. I ask her what went wrong, and she shrugs her shoulders. I shrug back. Neither one of us knows. We are bored. She is ready to move on.

"I feel lonely all the time," she says. "I don't know why."

"I know, we planned this wedding and it took over our lives. It seems like we have nothing to do now that we don't have to plan."

"I miss planning together," she says. "I miss the times sharing ideas." I nod. We down our vodka, and she pours us both another shot.

"Listen," I lean towards her. "I don't have any hard feelings. We part ways mutually, happily. But I'm wondering, what are you going to do with that ring?"

"This," she says, hoisting her finger vertically. "It's yours." She throws her hand in my direction, as if it were a used tissue. I unscrew the ring from her finger and slip it into my pocket.

"I just don't understand," I say.

"Neither do I," she says.

SLUT

I vacuum the house at precisely 8:00 each morning. At 9:35, I scrub the counters and wipe the stove. At 9:45, I sweep the kitchen floor. I sit in front of my computer at 10:00 and play solitaire. At 12:30, I make my tuna fish on toasted white, with a side of chips and a day-old banana. My husband wakes up at 11:00 and reads the paper until I begin lunch. Then the smell of my tuna fish on toasted white scares him off into the den. He's never been much of a fish man.

I can't help him; my husband has his own cycles and routines. Allan is fully retired. I'm quasi-retired. I still occasionally do some consulting work. I leave Thursdays open for these types of activities. I maintain Friday as a buffer. At 1:00, I run the dishwasher. At 1:05, I water all the plants in the house. At 1:25, I avoid making love to Allan, explaining that Charlotte will be home soon. At 1:45, tired from justifying my snub, I return to solitaire.

Then our daughter prances in – careless, selfish, and starving for attention – this occurs anywhere between 2:20 and 2:28. She is inconsiderate of our schedule. She wears those skanky skin-tight shorts. She wears slutty skin-tight tank tops, and platform shoes with straps that snake up her calves. Her mock-Obsession perfume pollutes our well-maintained atmosphere. Her barrage of cell-phone blips and pager bleeps send us scurrying away. Then she insists on e-mailing every friend in the greater tri-state area and beyond, while inhaling bags of cheese popcorn and Tootsie Rolls, and blasting the latest thrash metal (although, in the end, this may dissuade the call-girl garb). This girl eats like a linebacker. Give her six months and she'll be a heifer. She'll have more chins than her whale cousin, Sheryl. Charlotte is a locust run amuck, the bane of our existence.

An hour later, she's out the door. She's been gone since seven. Now it's eleven thirty, and I've been calling every friend in her phone book. She is nowhere to be found.

RANTS AND RAVES

*

Last Saturday, Charlotte and I walked the neighbor's dog, Sal. Unbelievably, the neighbor's entrusted Charlotte with their house and three-car garage! They told me Charlotte seemed like a very responsible young lady. Little did they know she'd be on her back on the master bed, inhaling pipes full of funky weed while boinking the lacrosse team. This is perhaps an exaggeration, but I doubt it's far off. Every time I looked out the window, a strange car was parked in the driveway. During our walk, I saddled her with this question: "So who are you screwing over there?"

I tried to convey to Charlotte all the parental clichés – that I'm her mother, that despite her developmental state she is still my responsibility. I followed this with another pointed question: "Do you have a boyfriend?" What I was looking for was some sense of self-sufficiency. If she could maintain a boyfriend, at least she was *organized*. I paid my way through college. I worked my way up the ranks to colonel. I transitioned nicely into civilian life. *All by myself.* Allan was peripheral. Somehow, I have failed to teach Charlotte the steps to inner toughness – or perhaps she learned her milquetoast demeanor from Allan. Perhaps the steps are too subtle for me to spell out. Then again, perhaps she just doesn't get it.

"Why would I want a boyfriend, Mom? I'm sixteen. What is it with you? Do you want me to get pregnant or something?"

"Believe me," I said, "you can get pregnant without having a boyfriend. And the way you dress, it won't take long."

Charlotte crossed her arms, and fixed her face into blankness, refusing to talk, jostling the chain to fill the void. I decided not to press the issue…then. I would wait until I could *engage* her. I wanted a battle, not a massacre. We walked by a playground. Three and four-year-olds slid down the sliding board, kicking up mulch, and bolting back up the steps to give it another shot. A mother swung her giddy child on the swing set. Two little girls in yellow dresses held hands and picked dandelions. I missed the days when I had more quality control over Charlotte, when she wasn't resistant to my every suggestion. I missed *feeling* maternal instead of merely indignant. I missed the sensation of Charlotte cuddling up to me in

the car, or curling up with me for a nap. I missed oneness.
I noticed Charlotte watching too. I wonder what, if anything, she remembers from her youth. Sometimes I wish I could hypnotize her into recollection, and permanently plant my memory there. As we walked past, I lifted my hand to pat her shoulder, but Charlotte jerked her head around and stared at my hand. I pulled a tendril of hair behind my ears.

From Charlotte's perspective, I suppose I am eccentric in my own way, certainly not easily relatable to someone her age. I feel *unsafe* if a dirty glass mars the sink, or if a skin of dust covers the bookshelves. I feel unsafe if the sheets aren't made. I believe in courtesy, elegance, and grace. I save every penny I can, and don't risk my life or limb on weekend excursions, much less vacations. I'm a relic.

Charlotte claims I am a hypocrite; I am responsible for her behavior, she says. I am the one who raised her. If she's a slut, then there must be something in me that's slutty, she says. This strikes at the heart of every mother's fear. Even though I bought her skimpy clothes, or gave her permission to do so, I can't validate her principles or lack thereof. Otherwise, I suppose I wouldn't buy her *any* clothes these days. What, are they *trying* to make girls into the image of disease-ridden, heroin-addled streetwalkers? Still, I'm not responsible for the world or our culture. If I was, I could change it. Yet, what has happened to elegance? What has happened to courtesy? When I ask Charlotte questions of that nature, she shrugs. Perhaps I am setting a bad example for her by not working full-time; I question the value of retirement sometimes. Maybe I should wait four more years. But internally I have nothing left to give the world. I'm through. I cope; hatred does have some positive value. No matter how hard I try, I can't let women off the hook. You see these fish-stick whores on the cover of *Vogue* and *Cosmopolitan*. That's what women aspire to now. I may have been a feminist sympathizer at one point; but the women who are dumb enough to follow suit have to stick up to their end of the bargain now. A bunch of ignorant little girls and idiotic waifs! I hate these skinny bitches who flash their tits like no tomorrow and screw their way up the ladder; I hate the vapid teenage sluts who mimic them; I hate these professional women who swank the illusion of grandeur (while spiting house-bound mothers); I hate the house-bound mothers for keeping to themselves in their mini-vans and gated communities; I hate the dykes who try to convert the unfulfilled to their path (as if it's that much better on the other side). This is not an easy time to be a woman.

Since her housesitting arrangement ended, Charlotte has been staying out later and later, but this is ridiculous. I call Aaron Cohen, then Teresa Grant, and she's nowhere to be found. I am about to dial the police when I hear the front door open. She runs upstairs before I can even make it out of the kitchen. I hear her bedroom door slam, and music blare. It's fight or flight time.

Allan has fallen asleep in front of the golf game. I jostle him awake in the nuclear glow of the television. Horrible as it is to say, if Allan were run-over by a truck tomorrow, I would be secretly relieved. I would mourn the end of an era, but who wouldn't want a new lease on life? Who doesn't want release from their bonds? Wipe the board clean. On the news yesterday they interviewed Gulf War widows. Tenth anniversary claptrap. I envied them. I could be like Charlotte, catting around with whatever men I please, wearing skimpy clothes, staying up to all hours e-mailing friends and eating junk food. As it stands, I'm stuck with the commitment I made when I was barely legal. Perhaps Charlotte has a point and someday they will look back at our dictated monogamy and scorn us.

Allan isn't much good. I tell him Charlotte is home, and I ask him if I should confront her or let it wait until the morning. He struggles to keep his head vertical. He shrugs, and curls his feet under a pillow.

"Do you want me to go talk to her?" His voice is rasped and mumbled.

"No," I say. "I just wanted your opinion. I'll wait until the morning." Despite my self-sufficiency, I think I wanted backup on this one. Allan isn't ready for backup. I decide I'll wait until the morning.

Allan stumbles upstairs to bed. My whole routine is thrown off now. Because of Charlotte, I will have to be bleary-eyed tomorrow when I vacuum. As a result of her inconsiderate behavior, I will miss spots on the rug. Then I will do a sloppy job of wiping down the counters. It will throw my whole week out of whack. No. This is not okay.

    I turn off the lights downstairs, and check the doors to make sure they are locked. I sit at the kitchen table in the dark, watching the moon light pool in the backyard. The stars are barely visible in the light-polluted sky. It is a night for romantics, not war. With this moon, sneak attacks would be destined for failure. Oh well. Then failure it is. I get the old skeleton key. Her door will pop open clean and true. She will be shocked. That's one thing I have going for me. I sigh and wheel the vacuum out of the closet and lug it up the stairs one by one.

The Phrenologist

I say why rent when I can live on and on at a perfectly tidy service station, without the oil and gas and all of that messiness, of course, but the windows are nice and boarded up and safe since nobody but nobody knows I'm here or there or anywhere, and I don't take up much space anyway, and I'm a neat-nick, so I take good care of the insides. Nobody knows, I guess, or I guess I hope, and if nobody knows where I am, that's fine and dandy, since I'm a writer, and being a writer, I need time and space and peace and quiet and law and order, all of which are fairly difficult to come by when you live in Dundalk and work at the tunnel, which is what I do and where I live, but not who I am, since who I am is really and truly a metaphysical question, and like all or most metaphysical questions, it is unanswerable, or what have you. The important part is the space I have, and the time, and even at work I have time for me, and my ideas, which are really what got me into this whole situation of sorts in the first place.

I came from a place that will remain nameless, and I did go to a university that will also remain nameless, but also I had certain difficulties, even though the important part is that all the while I longed for something indefinable despite the certain difficulties. As far as childhood goes, my parents were fine parents, and we spent many fine hours of my formative years together. However, once these longings began to seem more important, my parents (who were good parents) didn't know how to be good parents anymore, all of which has nothing to do with the fact that we are no longer continuing to share fine hours of my formative years, since my formative years are over and done with, and we don't see each other anymore for several more or less compelling reasons – more being that I am now very devoted to my various hobbies and goings-on, and less being my parents don't exactly live close by, and don't live far away either, which makes becoming excited about the prospects of seeing them in the place that will remain nameless rather muted and difficult for me to process.

I am not really secretive, since if I could I would knock all the plywood off the windows of the service station – which (thank God) has little to no heat or electricity – or the like, but is still comfortable for me, since Leonardo da Vinci didn't have heat or electricity either, and I have plumbing, which he didn't have. So let's put things in perspective. I think about that when I sit on the service station toilet to urinate, and then when I'm urinating, which isn't always easy, I repeat the title of Franz Hall Gall's multi-volume work over and over until it comes: "Lehre Über Die Verrichtungen Des Herrns, Und Über Die Möglichkeit, Die Anlagen Mehrerer Geistes – und Gemutseigenschaften Aus Dem Bau Des Kopfes, Und Des Schedels Des Menschen und Der Tiere Zu Erkennen." And then I repeat it over and over again until it comes, and then I can be at peace again in the service station.

Some people say you have to love and cherish your parents and sisters and brothers forever and kiss the ground they walk on, and feed them stringed spinach and rice pudding when they are immobile with their broken hip and their spinal condition of varying degrees. Since I am a writer, I can be more concerned with more important things like writing a sentence until I get it right, because I can't seem to get it exactamundo, and until I get it exactamundo, I can't exactly go on to the next sentence, not to mention paragraph. The sentence I'm stuck on is the first one on page seventy-eight of book one of my trilogy, and right now it reads: "The hair, the wind, the wind in her hair – these sensations rippled through her like sonar."

Obviously, this is not exactamundo.

I have been writing and rewriting this sentence for going on three years, and every time I think I've finally got it exactamundo, I realize the sentence is not exactamundo because it's riddled with soft and squishy things, which I loathe, and then I have to stop writing because I get upset that my prose is filled with soft and squishy things, as opposed to hard and firm things, and then I get upset at my writing abilities, which are merely on hold, but also at my capacity to concoct a sentence that has the correct tone and function at this place in the story – which is another thing since the story hinges on the primary female antagonist's decision to exile herself from society and become invisible, and be alone from society, which she hates, though she never had the capacity to say so until she met another woman character – though I hope for God's sake that I can avoid any lesbian overtones, which are always difficult to avoid for various and sundry reasons. All of which is fine and dandy, except for the fact that I don't want to write a story about a character who shares even the slightest resemblance to myself, though the similarities are superficial, and I found myself more and more loathing my protagonist and her woman friend, and all women characters for some irrational reason, which was, I suppose, a sort of crisis point for me, and which lead me to my current and over-riding interest – phrenology – which is how this story started in the first place. Now my over-riding interest is preying on my former and waning interest.

Another consideration is this: here I am, writing a story about writing a story (or not writing a story), which was always something I wanted to avoid, and now here I am doing it, and loathing myself for doing it at the same time. Yet it continues. Suddenly my life itself seems down and dirty, and I don't mean just the abandoned service station, though I'm sure it doesn't help. It just seems unclean all of a sudden – being a writer and writing and writing about these sordid characters with their sordid fantasies, and fantasy is the key here – I want something larger than fiction, something like truth, which takes us back to Gall's multi-volume work and the over-riding interest, which is what I think about when I'm at work seventy-five to eighty-five percent of the time, and even when I'm not thinking about my over-riding interest (which doesn't include sticking my hand out like an orangutan and accepting folded and crumpled one-dollar bills), I'm thinking about thinking about it, or just waiting to think about it, like pressing the pause button until I can continue the movie – except when I continue the movie, sometimes I'm right where I left off in that place that's not a place, a toll booth in the middle of the highway where I stand all day taking the folded and crumpled one-dollar bills, and other bits of debris that drivers think I might be amused to collect according to my whims – Legos, old

Christmas ornaments, Matchbox cars, condoms, burning cigarettes, bits of stale cake and bagel crusts, old Kleenex and banana peels – all of which is groovy-two-shoes except unbeknownst to them, the moment they place their debris in my hand is the exact moment when the camera comes into play, taking a picture of their license, and earning them a none-too-pleasant fine.

What I've done to make this job bearable – a job I acquired precisely so I could hold a painless but brainless position to give me the mental energy for my craft and art – writing – is to etch a sign (without the consent of either the state or immediate supervisor) on my teeth that says "free phrenology." Since I never smile outside of the booth, nobody knows but the driver and myself, and this has, on a side-note, elicited some wild and wooly responses such as "Who's got phrenology locked up? And "Lady, you're not examining my phrenology for no amount of money." One lesson I've learned from working with the public is this: the public is off its rocker.

Sometimes though I'll get lucky. I'll get some wise guy who wants to try the free phrenology, and after I sort out the ones that get it confused with pornography, I run my hand over their face and hands to detect any elevations or protrusions, or protuberances, then I take their picture with my nifty-thrifty Polaroid from 1984 that still works fine, and then after it develops (which usually includes fifty-five seconds of uncomfortable sighs and coughs, minus the beeping and honking from the line in back of Mr. Wiseguy – not that they matter) I take out my magnifying glass and examine their head for protrusions and protuberances one more time, and then I jot down some basic characteristics that I can deduce in the available time at hand on my index cards that I always carry with me, and then I hand the card to Mr. Wiseguy. I'll tell him, for instance, that his protrusions indicate that he has a high impulse or propagation or a sense of cunning and in this way perhaps he will try to find out more about the funny word that begins in P and H and perhaps he will even run across Gall, though I doubt it. More likely, he will stuff the card in his pocket and roll his weed into it, and smoke it while carousing with numerous ladies of leisure in some seedy Thai massage parlor, or use the card to blot out some blood on his face the next morning after he cuts himself shaving from too much vodka and speed, or he'll use the back of it to write the phone number of some hit man in Philly who can waste his ex-wife who's pushing the child-support issue, whether or not he's employed. Or maybe he'll cuss me out for telling him he has protrusions, though he probably won't. I rarely get a tip.

This is just the window-dressing. When I really and truly want to get down to business, I have to get more than a picture, which is why I spend an hour a day walking down by the industrial zone, where I've found a total of seven bodies to this date and taken the necessary specimens where I can perform further necessary operations and procedures in a safe environment away from industrial waste and smog, where oftentimes my operations and procedures can get muddled in the smog and random debris. When I really and truly want to get down to business, I have to dislocate a head and try to map the cartographic layout of the cranium, which involves what Gall calls organology, or what other less brilliant (not to mention professional) phrenologists called head-reading, and this involves all kinds of gore and skillful skinnings, and gruesome processes, but which despite the gore and gruesome processes are worth it, because now I have six complete cartographic layouts, and I am completing the seventh, and this is important work, since purchasing another phrenologist's cartographic layouts – if possible at all – would involve thousands and thousands of dollars, which I don't have what with my toll booth work and my service station and all, which sometimes, for a nanosecond, makes me wonder if all of this is worth it, until I think again in the nanosecond directly following the first nanosecond and realize that, yes, it is worth it, and that, yes, I am a writer who likes to skin people's heads and draw on them, which is what all of this comes down to, and then the third nanosecond comes and I realize that this is what I am meant to do, in my life, as my calling, and then I go back to the skull and look up at my mapped craniums on my cranium shelf which I stabilized with some cinder blocks and bricks, and I see how those heads, which were formally useless, are now useful to the world, and when this realization comes, I smile very, very widely.

*

I hardly ever dream of anything but my projects, but last night I did. I had a dream that York came to me, and when York comes to me, usually this means that something unexpected is going to happen, and when something unexpected happens, this usually means that I'm going to be unhappy, because unexpected usually equals bad. The dream started as one of my ordinary dreams: my latest cranium was talking to me and telling me all of its interesting facets and capacities – valor, disposition for coloring, sense for sounds, comparative perspicuity, theosophy – but then York came out of one of the protuberances in the area of mechanical skill (which in itself is strange, since I thought if anything like that happened, it would happen in metaphysical perspicuity), and he was in the nude, which is often how I saw York, and his penis and testicles made an elephant's face that did all the talking, since York's own head seemed lifeless and devoid of thought or energy. The elephant lifted its trunk and began speaking about how I would receive a visit from my sister, and that she missed me terribly and has been trying to contact me, since I was in an unknown place to her, and she was used to at least seeing me at dinner time when we were younger, and now she's pregnant with her second child who I haven't met, much less the first.

I thanked York for this helpful information, and then York turned into a bundle of thread and yarn, and he unwound himself slowly, with the elephant trunk still in place. Meanwhile the elephant kept talking and talking and talking, and I can't remember what he was saying, but it seemed important, and I nodded, and when I nodded, I woke up and then realized that I should go back to sleep to see if York unwound himself all the way, since I wanted to see what would happen to the elephant within that big pile of yarn. But I couldn't go back to sleep. Then I thought about how York was my last manfriend, and the fact that there were many more before him, before I became a writer and phrenologist, and before I left my parents' house and moved off to college, where I became celibate and refused to touch or be touched, but I don't often think of those times, and I don't intend on starting now, for better or worse.

RANTS AND RAVES

*

Chief Joseph of the Nez Perce is one of the more formidable and noteworthy examples in the world of phrenology as a result of the wideness of his skull at the ear level (showing the trait of destructiveness and strong perceptive faculties), and the general slope of his brow. The American Indians as a people were known for their excellent orientation and tracking skills, which is often reflected in a strong development of locality, and in addition to their strong development of locality, they often have a high degree of spirituality – all of this was present in Chief Joseph – and benevolence as well as a profound respect for nature. If he had the chance to see the skull of the famous chief, I assume Gall would find other more impressive characteristics present (even inventing more on a need-to basis) such as faculty for words and disposition for coloring, or sense for arithmetic and time (though this isn't known to be a primary trait of these peoples as far as I know), and I'm sure Gall would compare Chief Joseph's skull to that of his wax moulds and other human samples that he collected in much of the same manner as I do (though in a dramatically more tolerant society if I may say so), and if he had the chance, Gall would use that technique of his for dissecting the brain from below following the medulla oblongata into the brain, and tracing out the fanning fibers of the brain stem, but he didn't, because Franz the Second banned his lectures in 1801, and by all accounts was the indirect cause of the man's death. If I could dig up Gall's corpse, I would try his own technique on him, and I'm sure I would find every trait in the book right in those fibers. If I had a million dollars, I would buy Chief Joseph's skull and place it in an airtight translucent box of some undetermined material that wouldn't allow the skull to be touched or damaged in the slightest manner, and then I'd set it next to my samples to remind me of how far I must go to achieve the level of analysis that Gall and his disciples brought to their science, and then I suppose I'd put Gall's skull in there with Chief Joseph and let them keep each other company. It's pretty lonely when you're just an old shriveled skull.

*

My sister looks like any sister looks, whether she's pregnant or not, and she even walks (or waddles) like anyone else walks or waddles, and this isn't to say my sister is a bad sister – she's not a bad sister; she's a good sister – but my sister has her own peculiar ways and/or means, and these peculiar ways and/or means are more in the personality category than in the looks category, since she's pretty sisterly and womanly-looking with sisterly and womanly body parts and facial expressions and sisterly feet. But despite York's helpful prophecy, when I saw my sister at the tunnel, it was still unexpected. What happened was this: she drove right into my lane and fished around for her one dollar like everyone else, and couldn't see me anyway as a result of my hood and the tinted glass of her car and my booth, however, as soon as she looked up, she nearly dropped her money on the ground, which would have meant that either her or me (and she was pregnant, so it would have been me) would have to stoop down next to the car to pick up the quarters from the spit-stained asphalt, which neither one of us would have relished, especially her, since I'm sure she doesn't work in a job as down-and-out as this one.

After the near coin drop, the next reaction my sister had was to step out of her car and waddle over to me, where she offered me a long embrace in front of an aggravated gaggle of honking cars and headlights. She may have said niceties and pleasantries and additional words of kindness, but I was focused – honed-in you might say – on her belly, not what was in it, but merely the shape of the belly, the roundness, the protuberance, which made me wonder how exactly a head-reading of an infant cranium would work, or if it would work, since infants are part fish and chicken, or at least this is what I heard through pure hearsay. Then I said it: "Your stomach looks like a basketball." This made my sister react very strangely as she was hugging me and patting my hand and doing whatever sweet sisterly things she must have been doing at the time. I don't remember exactly what she said, but her forehead crinkled, and her brow browed, and the skin on her face warmed as if the sun was under her skin and rising above the horizon, which was the point at which I believe we became sisters again – not as if we weren't sisters before, but that as sisters we were more like not-sisters – and also the point at which she said something about something or other concerning the basketball. I was focused on the basketball at this point, however, and imagining the little baby basketball dribbling out from its basketball home and bouncing up and down the hospital making squealing, squeaking basketball sounds of joy.

I was finishing preparing number eight, which was my second female sample, and I was cleaning my warf saw and laying the sample on the workshop table below the other already mapped samples when I heard a clicking sound out and about the service station, which disturbed and bothered me, since clicking sounds certainly didn't come from inside the service station, and doubtfully came from outside unless it was a daw, or a caw, or a raven, or a crow, or a what-have-you type of bird. Luckily I do have a little peephole, which I carved out of the plywood using an awl. I peered out of the little awl peephole only to see a woman with five or six scarves wrapped around her neck flicking nuts or seeds around the service station, walking in circles and hopping all at once. Her scarves were red and orange mostly, but also yellow with a nice thick texture, which must have made them warm and cuddly in the winter, but this was July, and it was ninety-six degrees again for the fifth straight day, so I wondered. I almost wanted to peek my head out and ask her if I could buy one of her scarves, and then I did peek my head out and ask her if I could buy one of her scarves – "purchase" is how I worded it to be more formal and polite instead of rude and crude like my tunnel patrons. However, the scarf woman didn't answer, but instead continued to circle around the service station spraying seeds or nuts (seeds, I think) here, there, and everywhere. This would bring the daws and caws, I thought, which is not exactly the sort of thing I wanted around my samples. The woman's eyes appeared to be going in two different directions, and her ears were caked in mud or blood (or molasses maybe if she had some sort of kitchen accident), but I think it was mud or blood, probably blood. But the eyes were a bit on the disconcerting side, since one was off at thirty degrees and the other was closer to one fifty. Then the woman started singing this beautiful swaying song, which was about how the devil will come to capture his own and the stealers of the dead will be redeemed, and how places that house the dead will burn on the redemption day, but it all sounded quite pleasant and bluesy, which I liked, and I clapped when she was through and thanked her even if she didn't hock me one of her scarves. Oh well.

I followed the scarf woman over and over again, waiting for her to drop to the ground. One must always do the legwork, even if he or she doesn't turn out to be a sample. One never knows.

Why female samples? I believe Broca is right – that the female species (and I do believe we are a different species) is inferior – or at least ancillary – to the male for a variety of reasons, mostly having to do with the cerebrum. Gall once wrote to one of his disciples, "The heads of the women are difficult to unravel." This is where I pick up; phrenology is the gateway to truth about womanhood.

The next day, my sister came through the tunnel again. I don't know how she found my particular lane from the road, but she did, and when she did she gave me a nice long hug again and a package and she said that she didn't want me to open the package until I got home, and I said this was fine and dandy, and even though I wanted to open the package the whole time I was accepting crumpled dollar bills and clumps of change, I didn't because I didn't want to cause any trouble for my karma. She also said something about rescuing me, or something of the sort, but I was thinking about my new sample and how complex it was, especially considering it was at least a week old. At any rate, I placed the little package (which had a bow on top and was covered with goldish paper) next to my sample. After four or five hours of working on my sample, carefully performing my secret mapping procedures and processes, I did open the package. As soon as I opened the box I saw a small black instrument that began to beep and flash a little blue light. I wasn't exactly sure what it was, but since I didn't own a radio and since it did make a rather nice regular sound, I placed it next to my samples and continued to work to the gentle rhythm of the beeping and flashing. My sister is very thoughtful.

RANTS AND RAVES

*

When the first gentleman with a gun entered the service station with his friends, who also had similar shiny guns, I noticed right away that his nose was rather aquiline in arrangement, which usually indicates an absence of refinement, firmness, energy, and decision, which is why I wasn't afraid of his gun or general bearing, however, the individual behind him had what is normally referred to as a cognitive nose, which indicates strong patterns of thought, and an individual given to close and serious meditation, and this gave me pause, seeing as this is the sort of nose I have. Charlotte Brontë had a celestial nose, in my opinion.

I tried to tell the men about my samples, but their posture and gestures indicated to me they weren't really interested, though once they had me in their car, they seemed intrigued about King Baudouin of the Belgians, especially how the relative narrowness of the head compared to his height revealed him to be a man lacking of vital energy compared to the development of his mind. One of the men asked what a protuberance is, and I showed him directly on his head, and he seemed intrigued and interested, not necessarily in that order.

I suppose I should tell you all about the capture and the arrest, and my current living situation with men and women in white, and the bars, and the jingling keys, but it is rather clichéd all around, and not nearly as interesting as the fact that in the past week I have revised the sentence, which now reads as follows: "I caress the woman's large head, ignoring the body beneath." This was accomplished on the floor of the place where they are keeping me now, with my finger on the dust. I am busy rearranging the dust just so – I have much more to do here. Especially since I am now stuck on the next sentence.

The Pillar Ascetic

Truthfully, I live on the pillar, some sixty-one feet above the parched grasses and locusts below. The base and crown are of equal diameter: twelve feet by twelve feet, a perfect square resembling His perfection itself. Six plus one equals seven – the holiest number. Otherwise the pillar is ordinary stone. The platform is also twelve by twelve, and capped with a simple balustrade. I have not left the platform for thirty years, but tomorrow I will. The town carpenters are fashioning a ladder tall enough to allow me to climb down from my perch. They offered one of artificial means, but this will not do.

Besides my living conditions, I am an ordinary ascetic. I breathe the same air as you. I must eat and sleep, as you must. I must drink water, and attend to bodily needs. Yet on another level beyond, my needs are wants, and I leave my wants purposefully unfulfilled. This is the meaning of devoting your life to Him. Devotion implies selflessness, and for this I live in the clouds. One would be wrong to think that I do not have desires. My purpose in my descent lies in squelching.

Practically, my brethren hoist food and water to me, using a system of pulleys of my own design. Each morning at five, I receive my day's bounty: one loaf of bread, one lump of cheese, three pieces of fruit, and one wooden bucket of water. When I can hear the deliberate trolling of rope through the pulley system, I stop my prayers and gather my bucket from the prior day, drinking any remaining bucket water. Then I collect the new food and water, place it in the center of the platform, and set the used bucket in the container that will descend to the base of the pillar. Any bodily needs fall down to the base of the pillar. My kind brethren will clean the bucket and the base of the pillar and fill it with water tomorrow. I rarely see but the outline of their bodies in the dawn.

This is not to say my life lacks stimulation. When you live in the clouds, you can see the goings on all about you. When I constructed the pillar, there was no town. Since then, my followers and their converts have surrounded me in a circular district that rings my pillar at a circumference of five miles. I did not want them any closer. Many write letters to me, and I respond in turn. In some letters women offer intimacies. These I drop to the ground as not deserving of this holy spot.

Women have immense powers, and one must resist them with a hearty will, and with His assistance. The Holy Book shows women as they are. I do not wish any being harm. However, of my followers the women have, of course, been less obedient than the men. The women have attempted to rend me from Him, and for this I have harbored thoughts that I have eliminated.

After reading letters, I pray for hours, only stopping to eat or sleep. I will not explain or define my relationship to Him. It is everything.

I sat on a stump and prayed. It began with this. The stump provided me a difference. I was experiencing the world slightly differently than anyone else. I had lived in monasteries, and lived in hermitages. I was comfortable in silence, but there was something about the stump. I was a popular mystic. Followers sought my advice and wisdom. Perhaps the stump allowed me to be a bit above them all. I began directing my lessons from the stump, and meditated when they were not there. I couldn't leave.

Over time, I needed a larger pillar. I wanted to be higher above the others. I needed more solitude and more distance. I began building by the light of the moon, pillar stone by pillar stone, mortar and rock. I built instead of sleeping.

I thought of the sheep, and my father looming over them. My father would have me spook them to the river, or lead them into the pen. He could not afford a dog. I try to remember if I ever had a fleshly experience with a girl. It is all so long ago that at times I cannot seem to remember. Yet I think I am pure. I remember there was a cousin, and there was an aunt. My aunt used to kiss my forehead and pat my head. This is not fleshly though, according to His word.

I have desires though. I cannot deny this. There are these

followers, these women who offer themselves. I cannot say I have not been tempted by this. I have thought of their flesh. My mind has strayed many times. When this happens, I will deny myself a piece of fruit, or only allow myself half the bucket of water. If it happens twice in one day, I will fast. As a child, I used to fast often. My father said it was good for your body, and would make me do it to. I grew to like the feeling. I felt as if I was floating.

In their letters my followers tell me other ascetics have built pillars – at least seven or eight more. One even is a confirmed priest and a healer, and his followers come from thousands of miles to climb the pillar and seek communion and healing. Around each pillar there must be a town. This development has become overwhelming to me.

A woman named Zophar has written me many offerings, all of which I have declined. She has offered herself and her body to me. Often Zophar has offered to climb the pillar and offer her gifts to me. Each and every time I receive one of her letters, I drop it from the pillar with the others, where it floats to the ground. I never gave a thought to how these letters might be received once read by another.

At the usual time one morning, I heard the sound of the pulley. I squatted on the edge of my platform, awaiting my food and water, but when the container reached the top, a woman was inside. Her eyes were wild with envy and lust. She shrieked that she had to speak with me, that she had to touch my face. I let her touch my face, then I asked her to allow herself to be dropped back to the ground.

"My life is one of contemplation," I told her. "I cannot do what you ask."

Tears dropped from her eyes, and a look of frustration swept her face. However, she did go. I assume that same woman was Zophar. Now one of my followers has informed me that Zophar is to be jailed for many years for her scandalous behavior. I did not intend this. Jesus would not allow this; he would not allow Magdalene to be judged. How can I allow this? I cannot accept her offers, yet I also cannot allow these injustices. Tomorrow I must climb down from the pillar after these years, and I must speak to the judge.

*

The ladder is true, well constructed, and useful. I walk into town with the carpenters, since I know nothing of where the court might be or where to find this judge. People hold their noses as I walk by, though their eyes glow. I am ignorant of much of the world. The judge is a stern man, tall and thick-bellied, bearded to his waist. He hears my plea and offers to annul the case as a result of my forgiving gesture. I am heartened.

Since I am in the town, I offer to see this Zophar. I want to show her that I am just a man, and perhaps the visual sight of me in the daylight will repel her enough to alter her mindset. The carpenters take me to the prison where she has been living these past months. She walks out of the building and falls to her knees. She recalls my face. Over and over again Zophar thanks me for saving her, offering anything I might desire in return. She has not changed herself or her outlook. I tell her what I desire is to see her home.

"I have not seen a home for so many years, it seems that I might forget what one looks like."

She takes my hand, and I let her. She leads me down the street and into an alley, and through that to a tall building, and up the stairs to her home. She opens the door, and I can see it is empty. She has a bucket of water and three apples on a simple table, and a loaf of bread. Otherwise the room is unadorned. The carpenters laugh, but I do not know what to say. I nod to her and ask her to lead me back to my pillar. I thank the carpenters.

She touches my face before I climb the ladder. Her hands feel warm against my flesh, and for a moment I lift my hand to return her gesture. I stop myself, and climb the ladder, and when I reach my pillar, I can see her below, still watching me. I push the ladder with enough force that it falls to the ground.

There are so many prayers to offer to Him. Some days I am overwhelmed with my sense of duty and humbleness. I remember the selfishness of my youth, and how I owned at least four shirts. My life has been pared down to its essence, and I am in His service. This is not the way for all, but my way. These days I find desirous feelings enter my being less. As a result, I dream more. In my dreams, I float in the sky as the birds do. I float over the towns and all the pillars, over the followers and over foreign lands. Then I reach the sea, and I float over this. Everything is the same then. The sky is blue above me, and the sea blue beneath me. Then I am lost in the sameness, and I am content until I wake.

July Burn

When our friends invited us over for menudo, we went, even though we don't eat tripe. Faye and Thorn lived only fifteen minutes away, and it wasn't exactly difficult to drop by for a Sunday dinner in July. But my relationship with Thorn seemed to be on the outs, and I had to emotionally prepare myself for a visit. Pam couldn't stand Faye, and we both agreed that Thorn was worse for the wear as a result of Faye's compulsions – particularly as it manifested itself in her "art." If you want to know how I readied myself emotionally, think of all those scenes you've seen in boxing movies where the trainer pummels the pugilist's back until it is as loose as a down comforter. But Thorn said he had something to show us, and that we had to come quick.

Hug, kiss, hug, kiss, everybody forced smiles and clapped backs. We brought a bottle of the cheapest Chianti, since the drinks were the one aspect of the dinner Thorn didn't describe in excruciating detail. He considered himself a gourmand of the highest order, and maybe he was, but I'm perfectly content with a burger or lasagna, and Pam is too. I don't understand who he was trying to impress.

"Oh, good," Faye said, looking at the label. "Bertrand's." She grasped the neck of the bottle as if it were a flayed squirrel I downed with a pellet gun out back. I always forgot she didn't drink. She should have. They waved us into the living room.

Their apartment was definitely what most people would call odd. The first thing they did when they moved in was convince the landlord to let them paint the walls brilliant yellow – the store called the color "July Burn." On the blinding, sleep depriving walls, Thorn managed to mount his stuffed animal collection. When I say stuffed animals, I don't mean the kind twelve-year-old girls collect on their daybeds. Thorn wanted to be a taxidermist, but he was only a writer. So Pam and I walked into their living room surrounded by the marble eyes of fox, rabbit, hawk, antelope, lynx, crane, goose, weasel, and so on.

We hated this hobby of Thorn's, and we told him so. He defended himself by saying that the collection recalled the early twentieth century and the aristocratic tradition of taxidermy and exotic travel. Once I said, "That just makes me like it even less." Thorn responded by saying "If you don't like it, then fuck you. Nobody's asking you to like it." Yes, he could be childish, and I guess I could too. Truthfully, our relationship hadn't progressed much beyond college, although we were both thirty. But we adjusted: Pam and I were actually *used* to the mounted heads and stuffed creatures, however cruel and stomach-churning it seemed.

We were also used to Faye's paintings. The funny thing was that although she considered herself an artist, always referring to herself as such at parties and so on, she had only painted three pictures, all of them of the same plain yellow wall cloaked in a shadow from the left (Title: "July Burn in the afternoon?" We'll never know). All three canvases were ten by ten, and were, as she said, "unfinished." Yet, she didn't mind hanging them on the walls in eight-hundred-dollar nickel frames. She said the wall appeared to her in her dreams nightly, and she simply hadn't been able to capture the exact texture and tone of the wall in her three attempts. And this is what has consumed her for the past seven years? She could talk all night long about the symbolism of her wall paintings (wailing wall, wall of death, the chasm that separates ourselves from our deepest natures, and so on) but when it comes right down to it, she was in a rut the size of Oklahoma.

"Come into the dining room," Faye said. "That's where she is." Pam and I looked at each other in horror, fearful of the next turn. "She?" They lead us through the kitchen, where the menudo bubbled on the range (it actually smelled good), and into the dining room. There in a glass rectangle, in the far corner of the room, stood the skeletal remains of a woman, the rags of her sweater and skirt dangling from her bones. Above the casket, a placard read Mary Bollinger.

"Oh my God," Pam said.

"Isn't it exquisite?" Thorn bent closer to us for our reaction.

"I bet she *was*," I said. "It looks like she's dead now though."

"Oh," he said, shrugging. "I guess it is."

"*She* is," I said, irate that this was the reason we felt obliged to come over for cow brain soup.

"Isn't it beautiful? Unique huh?" Faye asked. "It's not every day you get to see a corpse in somebody's apartment."

Pam grabbed my shirt, saying she had to rush for the bathroom pronto. She mumbled she wanted to leave as she ripped away from me. I glared at Faye to say, "This is all your fault, you effete bitch." She beamed a satisfied smile at me, and smiled at Thorn. They seemed to actually enjoy shocking and humiliating us.

"Are you enjoying yourselves?" I said.

"Oh Jesus," Thorn said. "Don't get your panties in a twist."

"So this is art then?" I said.

"Look," he said. "Once you get past the fact that she's dead, it's actually pretty aesthetically pleasing."

"It really does add a lot to the apartment," Faye said. "Michelangelo performed surgical operations all the time. He thought everything was beautiful."

"He was studying the human body," I said. "You're not. You paint yellow walls."

"I think she will be inspiring in some way," Faye said. "She will add something to the apartment."

"No," I said. "You know what would add a lot to the apartment?"

"What's that?" Thorn said, smirking and pulling his hair back. He didn't want to hear my criticisms. My suspicion was that he and his ding-dong wife wanted me to just *enable* their offensive hobby, almost as if if they didn't get an outside reaction, the hobby couldn't exist. The year before, Thorn had grown his hair out and developed a fu-manchu beard, and rubbed lemon on his skin because he said it would make his skin darken. That way he could change races. "Asians *are* smarter," he said once.

"Plants," I said. "You need plants. It's like some kind of death museum in here."

"Who needs plants? We have animals. And now Mary."

"Jesus Christ, Thorn. You bring the dead into your house," I said. "Do you think that's really the best idea?"

"Who says I can't decorate?" he said. "Think of it as recycling.

Why waste a good body on worms?" Pam shuffled back into the room, looking pale. I could feel myself slipping into a wrathful flurry, which would consume the evening, along with any good will the evening might offer. I pulled back. Of course I was disgusted. What gave them the right to display this woman's remains as if she was their latest Kandinsky print? But what could I do? I looked at Pam, who closed her eyes at this point, and I bit my lip.

Dinner was actually pleasant, once we got past the corpse. Of course Pam and I insisted that we sit in the living room, away from the dead body, and I stayed away from the menudo, helping myself to a can of tomato soup instead. But in general, everyone was on their best behavior after we left the accursed dining room. We ate sitting on the couch with dinner trays over our laps, drinking wine out of their crystal.

Sensing that the evening could turn sour if the conversation reverted back to Mary, Faye talked about her job inspecting the houses of work-a-holic yuppies who wanted to be sure their cleaning people were doing a good job.

"It's too much. You have people hiring me to check up on their hires. This one couple I inspect for sleep in their offices during the week. They work twelve-hour days, 'so what's the point of coming home?' they say."

Faye had a different job every month or two, and I hadn't heard much about this one. She seemed to like nitpicking with other people's stuff even more than her own.

"They are more anal than I am," she continued. "I found a dust bunny under the dresser of one, and they went ballistic. They fired the maid service and sued them for a refund of their last two weeks of payment. Can you believe it?"

Pam nudged my shoe. I smiled painfully. What we couldn't believe was that a woman who had spent the past seven years painting the same thing could criticize anybody's sense of particularity. But the hypocrisy was just the tip of the iceberg. I didn't mind if Thorn was a trucker who hated truckers, and a writer who hated other writers. What bothered me about Pam, and increasingly about Thorn as well, was their lack of self-examination.

They seemed to bolster their own self-worth while undermining others'. Right before my eyes they were becoming vain, snobbish, priggish oddities.

After dinner we played Aces, and talked about what we could. Pam stayed close to me and feigned interest in Faye's culinary descriptions. Thorn confessed he was still working on the same story after twelve months (it was only three pages long). To distract myself from my own frustration at that point, I asked him where he bought Mary. Thorn watched my brow knit with faux curiosity.

"I thought you didn't agree with the idea," he said.

"I don't. I don't. I was just wondering." Pam pinched my hand, and shook her head at me for bringing up the subject.

"Guy from North Carolina that I met on one run down there this week turned me onto this sort of gothic auction down in Raleigh. I went and bought her on Thursday."

"How much."

"Just a grand," he said. "That's all."

"That's all?" I asked. "Hell, why didn't you buy *two* people?"

"She's not a person," he said. "She's just a dead woman. Now if it were a man, it might be a different matter."

"I see," I said.

As we drove home, Pam and I swore we would never return to their apartment again.

But the next day Thorn called. Pam was still at work, thankfully. I was curious.

"I had a dream," he said. "Really scared me, man."

"What's that?" I said.

"Dreamt that the entire apartment building went up in flames, and Faye died. I survived, but I was burnt from the neck down."

"Jesus," I said.

"It's just a dream," he said. On his end I could hear the news. He never watched television.

"It's just a dream," I said.

"But uh, something else," he said.

"What's that?" His voice quivered and I got a sudden feeling of déjà vu and general weirdness.

"The doctor severed my head from my body and mounted me on a plaque in the hospital. They told me I would be their new receptionist."

I didn't really know what to tell him. It *was* a terrifying dream, but it didn't mean anything, and anyway, he's the one that bought the woman's skeleton. He would have to deal with his own conscience. He said Faye wouldn't be home until late, and he was starting to creep himself out. At that point he asked if I would come over for dinner – just me.

"Sure," I said. I wrote a note to Pam and blinked into the sunshine.

He still had enough energy that night to whip up ham and asparagus chakchouka, and once he began cooking, he stabilized himself again. We reminisced about the summer right out of college when we both got jobs selling fruit out of old pickup trucks. The business was a scam owned by some guy Harrison Levy, who changed locations every year. We thought it would be a good idea to work there, since we could write and read while we sold fruit. But the produce was too popular, and each time we would start a story or read a paragraph, we'd have to put it down and tend to a customer. I must have read all of *The Rainbow* that way. But we ate a lot of peaches. Since then I got into accounting and gave up the starving-artist life, but Thorn still worked a job that wouldn't take too much away from his writing.

These diverging paths colored our personalities, I told Thorn. I stopped writing for one, where he continued (barely). I became increasingly status quo, where he stuck to his so-called artistic principles. This was a nice way for me to say that I thought he was pretentious and I wasn't. In a deeper sense, however, what I realized was that our friendship was based primarily on shared experience. We had memories together that we all too often relived, but did we have any common interests? Did we really have a burning urge to share our time together? I don't think so. So why should our friendship continue? Mostly because I didn't have a reason to not want it to continue.

"I don't know," he said. "Part of me wishes I could find some distance on marriage. I have always wanted a bubble where I could be self-sufficient with my wife and nobody else would be necessary. I got what I wanted."

"But that's the contradiction," I said. "If you were 'self-sufficient' you wouldn't need anybody. It's the wrong word."

"Whatever you want to call it," he said. "It doesn't matter."

"I've been thinking. You know, I, uh, I just don't relate to you as well as I used to," I said.

"Yeah, I know you don't," he said. "But that's fine, isn't it? Do we really need to relate?"

"Whatever you say," I said.

"It's fine," he said.

When I got home, Pam was already there, talking to a friend on the phone about Thorn and Faye. As soon as she saw me, she told her friend she'd call her later. Moths pinged against the lights outside.

"Hey, listen," she said. "I talked to Faye today at work."

"And," I said.

"And she said that they are having second thoughts," Pam said. "They're having bad dreams, stuff like that."

"That's what Thorn was telling me," I told her. "I want to poke around a bit." I didn't tell her I went back over there.

So I did a bit of genealogical research on this Mary Bollinger. Took forever to track her down, but it turns out she was an Appalachian farmer's wife born in 1896, who died in 1927 of pneumonia. Not a whole lot is known about her life, other than the fact that she was married to a man named Heinrich Newland, who went on to have six more wives after her. Each wife died of different causes.

I called Thorn to tell him the next day.

"I had another dream," he said. "This time all the light bulbs in the house burst, and I kept finding pennies all over the place. On the rug, on the table."

"Did you find any in reality?" I asked him.

"No," he said.

"Then it's fine," I said. I told him about the genealogical information, some of which he knew. He didn't know about the husband's life after Mary.

"Thorn, don't you think it might be a good idea to return Mary to North Carolina?" I asked.

"It's not like the guy has an exchange policy," Thorn said. "She was just some poor woman."

"Forget about getting your money back," I said. "How about getting your sanity back? I mean, a thousand dollars is a good price for sleeping well." He said he'd think about it.

The next morning, Faye called me, saying that Thorn locked himself in the closet and wouldn't come out. She asked me to come over as soon as possible. When I got there, sure enough, Thorn was in the closet. I approached the door and I could hear him panting inside.

"Hey, Thorn," I said. "It's me."

I just heard a low grunt, followed by a moan, and then a "go away." But after half an hour, I prodded Thorn to come out and face the music. His hair was disheveled, and heavy bags hung from his eyes. He looked buggy and wired. I sat him down and made him drink a cup of coffee. I told Faye I would handle it. I asked him to tell me what was wrong. He said he couldn't sleep all night, and then he must have fallen asleep, because the next thing he remembered he was dreaming.

"What was it this time?" I asked.

"I had this dream, man," he said. "It was so vivid. My head was on Mary's body. I was very aware of what was going on around me, you know. I knew everything. And these mice kept approaching the casket, and they found a hole at the bottom. I was just standing there and I couldn't do anything. These mice were crawling all over me, and then they started to bury into my body and eat my organs. I couldn't move at all or anything. It was so real."

What do you say to something like that? I should have told him that this was what I predicted all along, but instead I just listened to him talk about his fears and anxieties. I was a psychologist, except I wasn't getting paid. Then, when he was better, and Faye was back in the room, I told both of them that if they didn't take this corpse and put it back where it belonged, I was out of their lives for good.

"I've had enough of this bullshit," I said. "I don't think a friendship means you have to accept everything no matter what. Be reasonable."

They looked at each other and hesitantly said they agreed.

The next day, we all drove for North Carolina. The trip was grim. Thorn and Faye held hands and wanted to hear Leonard Cohen and Sonic Youth. Pam and I didn't. We argued about everything. Off the interstate we took an exit, and found a patch of woods screaming with crickets and cicadas. We dug a hole silently. We didn't speak a word. When we were done, Mary was buried near an oak tree in the northern part of North Carolina. It wasn't home for her, but it was a lot better than before. Then we turned around and drove back.

A couple of weeks passed before we spoke to Thorn and Faye again. Thorn said he was writing a story about the experience, and that the arc of the story would be that the friendship suffers as a result of this dead woman. I told him that sounded like the right plot. He paused and sounded hurt, saying that he didn't think that Mary was a problem for his relationship with me.

"Do you really think our friendship suffered?"

"I think you need to think about that a little harder," I said. I told him that Pam and I had been talking about cutting him and Faye out of our lives for good. "It wasn't so much Mary. It's a whole worldview that is just different," I said. "You guys see the world as your own canvas. I just think that's a bit intrusive. That's all. That's what this is about."

"Just because you were right doesn't mean you're perfect."

"That's true," I said. "But we're closer than you guys right now. Anyway, I'm just following my whims here. I don't really want to come over to your apartment right now. You and Faye creep me out."

That night I told Pam that I made the big step, and we celebrated with beer and hamburgers and fries. We haven't spoken to them in years.

Retreat

You must be methodical if you want to accomplish anything. This is why I am the way I am. I want to accomplish. In 2000, I am no longer in some transitional period, nor am I so driven and focused as to know exactly what I should want. Yet, I *am* driven and focused, and I do know *that* I want. I am twenty-nine years old, which means I've suffered my share of disappointments and loss, and of course have much more in store: more loss, more disappointments, more American drudgery, more apathetic wanderings in the name of "travel," more indignant soul searchings, more nights filled with bloodshot fears. This may sound startling, but I wish some larger, more powerful nation would just invade us. That would alter perspectives. That would inject some humility into our otherwise swaggering and self-indulgent ethos. I am bored. I am unusually usual.

Except what happened six months ago. My wife was walking across the street – no, a highway – at a crosswalk mind you, when an idiot – no, an ASSHOLE, a drunken-coked-up-piece-of-shit, in a ratty van with its muffler dragging on the ground sending sparks this way and that, hit her, slammed into her. Understand? The impact sent her twenty feet into the middle of the intersection. My wife. The love of my life. The woman for whom I renounced my position at GHS in Manhattan to move to this shit-hole area in the first place was transformed into a drooling paraplegic, and I had to hire a nurse to live with us and wipe the shit from her ass, dab the drool from her scarred mouth. All a result of this man, who was – of course – fine. After only a few years of finally escaping the tractor-beam pull of our respective parents, now I had to *pay* for someone to interrupt our peace. After years of struggle, after years of effort, scrimping, saving, filling my time with needless worries, "giving my all," some piece of shit in a piece of shit van destroyed all my gains. A man I never met. I would have felt comforted had it been a real enemy with tangible grudges. Then at least I could have felt defeated. As it stood, I felt more *deflated*, a victim to chance.

So what? Who cares? People suffer tragedies of a personal nature every day. What makes my situation so special? To tell you the truth…nothing. It's all a fucking grouse. After several weeks, I just wrote my wife out of my existence. I bought a cheap condo, and moved out. I started sending monthly checks and making weekly visits, but my wife was a person of my past. She was not mine any longer. As a result of the accident, she was a creature of medicine – her bodily parts probed and monitored. The leap in faith was too vast. I was not about to surrender my entire life. She had the nurse to take care of her now. Call me cold or evil. Fine. I had forfeited enough.

Then yesterday… I went for a walk around Lake Elkhorn. What happened? I'll tell you what happened. I walked down the path towards the boating dock. Children walked with their parents, and nannies pushed babies in strollers. Couples swung their hands together and held each other close. Teenagers cut school to make out in the woods. Old men walked their dogs by the water, and sons fished with their fathers from the bank. I followed a woman around the path.

She was speed-walking, with little pink two-pound hand weights pumping in her hands. Her leg muscles glistened in their vinyl sheathes. I had to hoof it to keep up with her. But I had to literally hold myself back. The way her hips wiggled, the way her prissy little arms pumped back and forth, the way her legs pivoted on the concrete and released themselves from their pivot – all of it seemed so prim and proper and uptight. All of the frustrations of the past few months washed over me: my shame and unconscious guilt, my sense of persecution and self-loathing, my emasculation. I wanted to rape this perfectly normal, probably nice person. I wanted to shove her face into the water, shred her ass-wiggling shorts, and ram her until she bled to death. I wanted to come into her dead body and bash her head in with a rock. And the woman wasn't exactly a knockout. She was squat and pudgy with a dimpled Shirley MacLain face. Yet, I was filled with the kind of rage that I never thought I'd feel. I was clouded by this anger.

I followed this woman all the way around the lake (she didn't notice), until I exhausted myself with my own intentions. I was startled by my own reaction, so I sat on a bench, under a stand of beech trees, and watched her thrust on into the shade. I realized then what I had to do.

All my belongings were at my condo, but I needed to be punished. So I moved back. I locked myself in the basement of our house, a dungeon – it felt like a place where sex criminals belong. Kathy didn't hear me come in, and likely slept in some semi-comatose paraplegic stupor. In the morning I could hear my wife wheel her way around the house, sniffle and cough (to add insult to injury, she had a cold). I built a ramp so she could get in and out, but unless Kathy sprouted new legs, she couldn't get at me down in the netherworld. Instead, she'd bellow down to me: "Open up!" "Roy, why are you hiding?" "Roy, I haven't seen you in two days!" "Roy, I need your help." "Roy, it's not your fault." "Roy, I don't blame you." "It's not your fault." "I love you." It didn't matter. I wasn't coming out. I wasn't going upstairs. I had the freezer, and the kitchenette from when we used to rent the basement out to that bitch Jenny Moore, who nearly trashed the place with her drug-addled friends, who smoked and spilled beer and spewed vomit, and God knows what else all over the place. Every night was orgy night at Jenny's. Only one of her friends was decent and likable – an older man, a P.E. teacher at the high school down the street. He used to tell me how he'd fantasize about the girls in his classes, how it'd take every muscle in his body to restrain himself from fondling them when they approached him in their titty-hugging-tube-top-and-biker-shorts-get-ups. "These aren't girls," he'd say. "These are women. It's a miracle I haven't been put away for rape yet." But he was friendly.

"We all have it in us," I'd say. "Men are animals."

"Hell yes," he'd say. "I have it in me for sure."

At first the P.E. teacher came to mind as a consolation: "Poor, poor me. I'm not the only one who has carnal urges." I would spend all day in the basement just thinking. I didn't want to read books. I didn't want to watch movies. I wanted to just ride the wave of my thoughts. I wanted to solve my problem. What would cure my affliction? What would bring me peace and solace? Then it came to me.

I still had a phone number for Jenny – her parents' number – and by calling I was able to acquire her newer number. I told them I needed to send mail to her that the post office wouldn't forward. "Won't forward?" they asked. "I'm not sure if she filled out one of those cards," I said. By calling, Jenny I was able to acquire the number of the P.E. teacher. By calling the P.E. teacher, I was able to arrange a tête-à-tête. He had no idea what it was about. I told him I couldn't leave the house, so he'd have to come over (I was willing to break my isolation for an opportunity of liberation, a potential break-out).

It was eleven thirty in the morning when he came, bald and ruddy-faced from the heat. After a morning of harassing me about everything under the sun, the nurse let him in. He found me in bed, lying there, gazing at the ceiling.

"Jesus Christ," he said. "What's going on, Roy?"

"What do you mean?"

"I mean, there's a nurse here who says your wife has been seriously injured. You are lying in bed, surrounded by filth."

I looked around. Used Kleenex. Shit-stained underwear. Clothes and sheets strewn all over the floor. Chicken skin. Moldy bread. Moldy turkey sandwich from a week ago. Crusty yogurt containers.

"I hadn't noticed," I said.

"Maybe we can, you know, sit out here, Roy," he said, gesturing towards the basement living room. I nodded slowly, and lifted myself from the bed. He watched me with trepidation, as if I was about to unleash some horrifying secret that he really didn't want to be privy to.

"What in the heck is going on here?"

"Accident," I said. "My wife was almost killed."

He expressed the appropriate amount of remorse and horror.

"Yeah, it's tough. Now the reason I wanted you to come here today…"

"Alex."

"Right, thanks. Want to offer you a proposition," I said. He leaned forward on the couch to hear this one. Alex the P.E. teacher was not one to be afraid to hear a rational proposition, whether or not its origins were deeply imbedded in murk. He was a real man's man, a man of honesty.

"Remember how we talked about the girls at your school?" It took Alex a moment to get a bead on my method of inquiry. All gestures of subtlety and social grace were beyond me at this point. I cut to the chase, and Alex clearly was taken off his guard. He thought I was going to ask him to help, and in a way I was.

"Who knows what I said when I was drunk," he said. "I said lots of things over here. Jenny was a wild one."

"Yep," I said. "Well, I remember you told me you found some of the girls attractive."

"Did I?" I realized without intending to, I vaguely put Alex in a defensive position. He must have been thinking blackmail.

"Yes, you did."

"Okay, I don't remember," he said, shifting in his seat and looking away. "What is this about anyway?"

I told him I wanted him to do me a favor, to which he gave the customary "it depends." Then I told him. At that he stood up. He looked me in the eyes and told me I needed to get professional help, real help. He looked around like a trapped animal. He made a sour face of contrition, wanting me to forget about him completely.

"It smells terrible down here," he said.

"Think about it," I said. "But I do remember the things that you said."

"But I didn't *do* anything," he said. "I do my job, and I go home. I may have revealed some things to you. That doesn't count for anything though."

"We'll see," I said. "Just think about it, Alex. It would really help Kathy and me if you would do us this little favor."

"Shit," he said.

A week later, I got a call. Alex said he liked his life, wanted to protect his way of living, would do what I asked to save that. That was the most important thing to him he said – protecting his own ass.

"Great," I said. "Come on over tonight."

When he got there, the nurse was gone. I had it all planned. I opened the door for him. I could hear Kathy wheeling around her room. I offered Alex a drink, and then another, and then another. This time it was more amicable: he had five beers. He said the only way he could do it was to get drunk as hell, and stumble out. We talked football, baseball, basketball. We made a bet on a women's college game (I couldn't have cared less). After his third beer, I couldn't hear wheels anymore. She was asleep. Then, when he was about to pass out, I flipped on all the lights in the basement.

"It's time to do your duty!" I said. "Get to work, buddy." I pushed him up the stairs. He was sweating, and his eyes seemed heavy. His face was red. I pushed him through the hallway, and to her door.

"Do it," I said. "I'm going to stand here and see it happen." He opened the door slowly. My wife's wheelchair rested next to the bed. The way her face was positioned on the pillow made me think of when we first met, how we used to nap together on the couch, how she would rest her head in the crook of my arm. I pushed Alex into the room, but he looked back at me. His eyes were mournful, diffident. Idiot. I waved him on. Then he caught a glimpse of her, of the whole room. A shudder washed over his face. I coughed. He pulled his shirt off first, grabbing the back first, the way a boy would. His fingers looked angry and intent as reached for his belt buckle. I could her breath whistle through her nose. He nodded. His hair bobbed in the dark silence, and he loomed over her.

WORKS-IN-PROGRESS

Knee-deep in the thick manly spirit of camaraderie, Abe and Mitchell bellyached that day about their lives, about their respective careers and romantic choices, their physical and psychological well being. Most of all, they paid homage to each other's manifest desires for something beyond the mere game they watched together, beyond the syrupy soda, and the mealy apples Abe brought from home. A thin vapor of rain fell on the field.

Abe tried to attend a baseball game once a month or so, and Mitchell usually joined him. Boy's night out. In February, Abe suggested that they purchase advance tickets for the games they might want to attend despite the hassle and possibility of an unforeseen rain cancellation. Abe still wanted to get their plans in order. Even if Mitchell said this destroyed the spontaneous spirit of simply saying "how about going to the game tonight?" Abe wasn't aware of any direct resentment on Mitchell's part – if Mitchell cared more for spontaneity than foresight, that was his privilege.

Yet, Abe realized later that perhaps some residual annoyance sparked the conversation that took place when Mitchell returned from the Men's room in the bottom of the 6th. Maybe he was annoyed that Mitchell *wasn't* annoyed, or that he wanted Mitchell to be more well defined. Abe nestled his Coke cup in the cup holder part of the cardboard tray.

"Let me ask you something," he said. "Have you, you know, ever thought about having an affair? Since you got married, I mean."

Abe pretended to pick at his fingernail as he asked this question to throw Mitchell from the pointedness of the query, or possibly to distract him, to put into practice something he remembered Woody Allen saying in an interview: "You have to mess up the joke, so it doesn't sound so jokey." Abe made sure he used his best "guy talk tone," as if he were asking Mitchell if he had ever seen a no-hitter in person, or a player hit for the cycle. Abe didn't want to appear as if he had an agenda.

"Wow, some question there Abe," Mitchell said with a wince, adjusting himself in the hard plastic chair. "I don't know. What about you?" The game was an eight to nothing blowout, and Abe hoped the rain picked up so they could go home and avoid the traffic congestion. There was nothing better to do than talk. "You're the swinger," Mitchell said.

This was exactly the response Abe wanted, for he truly didn't want to hear (nor did he expect to hear) about Mitchell's deep inner sexuality and sordid fantasies. He wanted to talk about *his* deep inner sexuality and sordid fantasies. Actually, what Abe really wanted was to force Mitchell to just listen, to confide in Mitchell as a kind of litmus test of their relationship: could Mitchell listen to uncomfortable revelations without ultimately becoming revolted or revealing them to his wife? Maybe there was an inevitable streak of cruelty implicit in this purposeful line of questioning, but Abe didn't like to think of it that way. Abe simply felt that his relationship with Mitchell could be stronger; Mitchell held back too much. Abe just wanted Mitchell to "let it go" sometimes.

Mitchell and Abe had become friends through Mitchell's wife, Kathleen. Kathleen and Abe went to school together at a liberal arts college in the south, and Abe and Mitchell struck up a friendship of their own over the three years Mitchell and Kathleen dated and later married. Abe and Gina weren't married yet, and they weren't engaged. By asking such a forward question, Abe didn't aspire to compromise either friendship; on the contrary, he thought a good secret or two would bolster their bond: Mitchell would carry a deep secret of his, which would probably not inspire Mitchell to share a secret of his own (at least right away), but simply to allow the knowledge and potential breach of trust to bring them closer. Either way, what Abe wanted was *closeness*.

"Yeah, well," Abe said, still pretending to pick at his fingernail. "I didn't mean to–"

"No, no. It's fine," Mitchell said. "It's fine."

"Whew," Abe said watching the mist whirl in the lights. "You know, to me it's not a big deal either way. I see all of this stuff as a type of experiment – marriage, kids, whatever. Whatever works for you." Of course, Abe didn't believe that laissez faire attitude for a second. There were rules; there was a right and a wrong. He wanted to appear non-judgmental to earn Mitchell's confidences, and he hoped Mitchell wouldn't see through him.

"Well, no, I'll tell you, I never have," Mitchell said. "It's not been something that, you know–"

"Well sure," Abe said. "That's the way it should be, right? That's what people say. For me though... I'm not that strong, you know. I'm pretty all over the place despite my, what would you call it? My domineering aspects, you know?"

"Yeah, sure," Mitchell said. "So you've..."

"Yeah, I've..."

"You've experimented, you say." Mitchell watched the next pitch tail in on the batter, and the rain falling with increasing speed.

"Well, no. Not exactly," Abe said. "I think about it all the time though. That's what I'm talking about," Abe said. He didn't want to reveal too much too soon. Take it slow.

"There is one friend," Abe said. "One buddy I have has this wife, and I'm telling you..."

"What?"

"She's incredible," Abe said. "And a little, no, *very* flirtatious. I mean, at a Halloween party a year ago... She was a little tipsy, but still – she grabbed my ass and kissed me on the mouth," Abe said, lifting his head, slapping his knee. "I could feel her tongue against my teeth. Bitch."

"Yeah?"

"She did this in front of her husband. Well, his back was turned, but I could see him as she did it. I think one of his friends told him, because I saw him watching me later. Big guy too. It felt pretty, I don't know–"

"Dangerous?" Mitchell leaned forward in his seat.

"Yeah, I think so," Abe said. "Nobody ever mentioned it though. It was just a moment."

"But he *is* your buddy, right? You said–"

"That's what I'm saying," Abel said. "I'm saying it's just a passing thought, but it's still there. I'm telling you though, there's not a day that passes that I don't fantasize about her. I mean, I have unfinished business. You understand. Right?"

"I think I know what you're getting at," Mitchell said. "Yeah." Good. That's all that Abe wanted. He wanted Mitchell to know what he was getting at.

"Why, exactly, did you just tell me those things, Mitch?" Kathleen asked. Mitchell rubbed her right calf. They sat arms and legs intertwined on the formal couch of the Motts' faux neo-classical house. The Motts were in Bermuda celebrating their anniversary for a week, and once again Kathleen was called upon to housesit.

"What do you mean 'why did I tell you those things?' I told you," Mitchell said.

"I mean–"

"Because Abe is our friend," Mitchell said.

Kathleen couldn't believe what she heard. Of course Mitchell surprised her, but that wasn't what bothered her. She simply didn't understand what compelled him to actually *tell* her. After all, Abe was an old friend; she felt close to his girlfriend; they socialized regularly. What was Mitchell thinking? Or more precisely, what wasn't he thinking? Mitchell was so stubbornly flighty and casual sometimes. He didn't think about what he was saying. Kathleen thought it was infuriating that he was so easily distracted, even self-absorbed; anyone who was not self-absorbed would have realized that they were saying things that shouldn't be said. Kathleen didn't want to know about Abe's fantasy life; in fact, she would have been more than content not thinking about Abe's sex life at all. Not only was she not attracted to Abe; she was married, and she didn't want the purity of her marriage compromised. She didn't want to feel sullied. She didn't want these intrusions into her relative contentment. Worse, why would Mitchell tell her these things if Abe had obviously confided in him? Even if Abe had fantasized about other women, or whatever he did, she was sure he wouldn't want other people talking about his inner life so casually.

In a way though, as Mitchell glibly yanked the curtain on the sordid corners of Abe's mind, Kathleen felt relieved on several counts. First, at least Abe hadn't had an affair. More importantly, Kathleen realized that at least she came upon, however indirectly, some inner knowledge of Abe. These days she found that she wasn't gaining more knowledge about the people in her life, only more information. This was knowledge. Maybe she was secretly curious, despite herself. Kathleen had become disillusioned by her relationship with Abe, and their waning emotional bonds. Yes, she still saw Abe often, but only in social circumstances, respective partners and spouses in tow.

Part of Kathleen still wanted the emotional intimacy with Abe they shared in their younger days. She couldn't help but wonder if their relationship had become scaled back to meet the demands of her married life. Hopefully the sexual tension inevitable in an opposite sex friendship hadn't influenced this lesser version of their closeness, but Kathleen suspected the worst. She hated the simple fact that society nudged all male-female friendships into the sexual sphere, despite her innocent intentions. It was a type of thought control, she thought, and her better instincts recoiled against this simple-mindedness. Yet, if she pushed the true nature of her relationship with Abe to its farthest extreme, perhaps there was a sexual element, even if it was only on Abe's end.

"I'm aghast," she said. "I am surprised at you. I didn't want to know about these things. What made you think—"

"Fine," Mitchell said, squinting. "Next time I won't tell you what's on my mind."

"That's not it at all," Kathleen said. "I just feel...dirty. Why would I...did he really tell you to reveal these things to me?"

Mitchell said he had to use the bathroom, which Kathleen knew was his out; he could come back five minutes later and change the subject and avoid confrontation – a disturbing recent pattern for him. If it was going to be that way, Kathleen decided she was going to walk around the house. Let him find her. They just arrived after all, and she hadn't seen the entire house. Kathleen walked downstairs: nymphs and dryads embroidered on pillows, Athenian wallpaper, wooden grapes in bowls, mirrored bathroom wallpaper. The whole house felt like some imitation of a Grecian-themed Las Vegas casino. Kathleen could hear the toilet flush and the water whistle through the pipes above her, and she knew she only had a few moments before Mitchell slouched out of the bathroom, talking about something he suddenly realized, or an idea for what they should do that evening. Anything but the confrontation itself.

Kathleen entered the crowning achievement of the first floor – the sitting room, complete with faux-Greek murals painted on the walls and cheap replicas of Grecian urns. Perhaps she was more upset by the raucous decor than the events of the day, but Kathleen realized she must do something to salvage her relationship with Abe. This indecent revelation could be a spur to a greater purity for her. Kathleen could reach out to this withdrawn (and possibly troubled) friend of hers who obviously was having difficulty reaching out himself. Kathleen felt inspired to do something, not necessarily in a vengeful spirit, but something to make Mitchell aware of her annoyance with his behavior. Perhaps she was being overly sensitive or too hasty in reacting to Mitchell's revelation, but part of her wanted to experiment with her own emotional reactions as much as his reactions to her. She wanted to challenge herself to help Mitchell realize that he needed to be more considerate, and observant, and understanding, instead of frat-boy gossipy and by the books.

Perhaps though it wasn't just his behavior that rankled Kathleen. Maybe Mitchell's closeness with Abe was at the heart of her annoyance. Now Mitchell was closer to Abe than she was. Was she being possessive? Competitive? All that Kathleen knew was that somehow adjustments would have to be made.

Gina wondered why they were acting so strange, as if the three of them were playing a little game from which she was excluded. Usually the dinners with Mitchell and Kathleen were so pleasant, but this one seemed to carry an edge of sinister foreboding, as if something was about to happen, some terrible accusation charged.

She reached under the table and squeezed Abe's knee, and as she felt his leg hairs through the thin cotton weave of his pants, she wondered if he still hated these small signs of public affection. When they first met each other, he wouldn't even touch her unless they were behind closed doors. But Gina liked to touch him regardless of what he thought. Luckily, Abe had lightened up some, but in her opinion, he was still a work-in-progress. The moral question was: should she want to change him? And could she change him anyway? All that Gina knew for sure was that she wanted to tear him away from Kathleen. Kathleen and Abe had been talking to each other that evening as if nobody else was around. So if she was monopolizing him (or he was monopolizing her) Gina wanted to do something to recapture his attention. If she could get a word in edgewise...

The one moment that made her sit up and take notice occurred after they had already consumed the main course. Abe and Mitchell talked about their childhood dreams. Abe had wanted to be a millionaire real estate magnate, and Mitchell said he had always dreamed of sailing around the world and winning recognition and fame. He realized that most records had already been established; nevertheless, it was a calling that for him was very strong. Kathleen cleared her throat.

"Well, you never took sailing lessons when you were young," she said.

"Are you sure I didn't?" Mitchell said, playfully tossing a napkin at her.

"Oh yes, I'm sure," she said. "Your mother said you were such a young dilettante."

"I was not a dilettante. I experimented," Mitchell said. "I tried all kinds of things to see what I would like and what I wouldn't like. This sailing dream lasted a while though."

"Even though you never sailed," Kathleen said.

"Yeah," Mitchell said. "But I *did* sail. Just not as often as you, maybe."

In Gina's opinion, the tone of the evening shifted at that moment. Mitchell's eyes narrowed. Kathleen crossed her arms in a seemingly defensive posture, and Gina watched Abe watch both of them with a sly smile as if he knew this was going to happen. Gina didn't understand.

"Are you implying something?" Kathleen asked.

"All I'm saying is you had more money. I mean, your parents–"

"If you really wanted sailing lessons, you could have had sailing lessons," she said. "My God, you act as if you grew up in a shanty town."

"My parents didn't live on a twenty-acre estate, like your

parents," Mitchell said. Kathleen just shook her head, but it seemed a shake of discouragement more than disagreement, as if she too was disappointed by the way the conversation shifted, or by his reaction to it.

"Wait a minute," Abe said, smiling.

"'It's fine," Kathleen said. "You're right, Mitchell. You are exactly right. I had it better than you. This makes you morally superior to me, and it makes me wrong."

Kathleen and Mitchell were picking an age-old fight, but Gina had never seen them snap at each other without their usual element of biting humor. Gina wasn't sure what Kathleen was after exactly. Usually her argumentative strategy was gentle appeasement, followed by sarcastic side-comments – especially when she talked to Mitchell. As a woman, Gina thought Kathleen was certainly arguing about something else indirectly. But what?

"Nobody can change their past," Abe said. He leaned back in his chair and held his hands behind his head, an act of magnanimous neutrality.

"True. Yeah," Mitchell said. "But your past affects you. I'm not going to be the kind of person with a sense that I can actually have all the things that I dream of. I just don't have that idea of, um, entitlement?"

"So, you think I feel entitled to be treated a certain way?" Kathleen leaned forward, her arms pressing against the table as if she was about to lift herself from her seat.

"You might be. More than me, I think," Mitchell said softly.

"Jesus Christ," Kathleen said. "There are plenty of things that I don't feel entitled to that are foisted upon me anyway."

"Sure, but that's–"

"For instance, information," Kathleen said. "We're talking about material things, and experiences, but what about knowledge? Huh? Some people feel they are entitled to know certain things. But knowledge isn't always–"

"Knowledge can sometimes be–"

"It's foisted upon me when I don't want to know something and I find it out anyway," Kathleen said. "This is not–"

"I see," Mitchell said, standing up. "I see what you are getting at here." He walked towards the bathroom. Gina watched Abe. His eyes followed Mitchell closely as Mitchell stood up and walked out of the dining room. A thin secretive smile opened on Kathleen's face, and she turned to Abe to change the subject. Gina scratched her leg, and took a drink of water. She didn't say anything. What could I do to help this situation? she thought. What can be done here? She didn't know where to begin.

"Do you think you 'foisted knowledge' on me?" Mitchell asked. Abe and Mitchell were sanding Abe's picnic bench in the driveway. While it was still summer, Abe wanted to repaint his patio furniture. It was Mitchell's idea to help him out. He felt guilty, of course, and wanted to help Abe understand that it wasn't a matter of breaking his confidence, it was more a matter of bridging confidence between his wife and him. The drop cloth was flecked with green paint, and pinned down at the corners with white paint buckets.

"I just told you what was on my mind," Abe said, sanding quicker. "I thought that's what people are supposed to do. But you know–"

"I know what you're going to say," Mitchell said.

"Well, I'm going to fucking say it then," Abe said. "I can't believe you told her what I told you. That was strictly boy talk. You want to trust a woman? Come on."

Mitchell threw his sandpaper into the grass, and stood up. "Oh, give me a fucking break, man. I tell my wife what happens to me. My inner life is her inner life. I don't think there is supposed to be this separation between my friends and her friends and my thoughts and her thoughts. Go back to the vows I had to take and you'll–"

"Vows? Those are just vows with *women*," Abe said. "When has that mattered to our friendship, that's what I'm talking about. What do you think this is all about?"

"Hey, I take that shit seriously," Mitchell said. "When you get married you 'become one.' I am one with Kathleen. If you want to tell me something, you tell her something. I'm going to talk about what's–"

"You know," Abe said. "You know that what you're saying is basically disregarding friendship. What you are saying is that your marriage is more sacred with all these vows and pacts – you're saying that is higher than a simple friendship. I think it's the other way around, mister. It's men versus women in this world."

"Who's married and who isn't?" Mitchell asked. Then he immediately regretted it.

Partially, Mitchell felt that he was in the wrong, but when Abe shined such a clear and harsh beam of light on his attitude, he felt that he had to do something about it – only he couldn't let Abe know that he felt that he did something he shouldn't do by any absolute standard. Mitchell thought that in this age, there was no outlet for secrets, or forbidden knowledge. Maybe I am just weak and can't keep a secret, Mitchell thought. He suddenly felt that he should go to confession, yet he wasn't Catholic, much less religious. Mitchell knew that confession was open to non-Catholics as well. He always thought that confession, by allowing an outlet for impurity, was one of the great inventions of Christianity. He wasn't going to apologize, but some release would help. Abe was still sanding the bench.

"Look," Mitchell said. "Things have been tough with Kathleen. Obviously. Give me a break, okay? Whether I should have or shouldn't have revealed what you told me is beyond—"

"It's not 'beyond' anything," Abe said. "I know you're not going to admit you were wrong, and maybe we can be better friends for this. Because we can, you know. But you're not better than me, or more entitled because you're married and I'm not."

"I don't know," Mitchell said. He picked up the sandpaper and placed it on top of the bench. "We'll see."

"You have to realize that you can have relationships with other people that aren't filtered through your marriage," Abe said. "You know what I mean?"

Mitchell just stood there, watching the paint flecks fall from the bench.

Mitchell took a walk. The path around Centennial Lake was two and a half miles long, and he walked around it twice, thinking. The more he thought about it, Mitchell didn't want to go to confession, or anything of the sort. That seemed like just a panicked reaction outside of his normal procedure for dealing with a crisis. He would rather take a walk and think. He watched two young girls throw bread to the ducks as a mother watched. An elderly couple walked down the path shoulder to shoulder.

However, Mitchell did want to come to some kind of peace. If his wife and friends were trying to change him, maybe that meant he needed to be changed. That was a distinct possibility. Yet, as Mitchell walked around the lake looking at the ducks and the picnickers, he realized that he'd rather go with the flow, without trying to judge other people, and allow them to try to mold him if they could. At the same time, he'd rather not try to mold others, not because he thought it was morally wrong or repugnant, just because he didn't want to waste the effort in doing something that was inevitable: you can't help but influence others in some way.

We are all works-in-progress, Mitchell thought. That's something that the moralists forget. Abe does have a point, Mitchell knew. He did allow himself to rank his relationships in a way, but that was his decision ultimately, and if it negatively affected his relationship with Abe, then it negatively affected his relationship with Abe. Part of him had to stick to his guns, and handle his life in the way he saw fit, rather than accommodate another person's code of honor. I have to do things my way, Mitchell thought. Mitchell could see Abe's code of honor though. He could recognize it and respect it even, but there has to be a line drawn somewhere, he thought. He was ready to start drawing it wherever and whenever he could.

Man to Man

Okay, okay, I'm talking. I'm talking. Put that away. Hold on. It's a good story. I'm talking.
 Lookit, what got the whole ball of wax rolling was that I want to be a kept man. You know? Sick of the grind. I'm sick of competing with bombshells in power-suits. I want to loaf around my house in my slippers all day, sip lemon water, listen to Bobby Blue Bland on vinyl, make split pea soup in my boxers. You have to admit, it's worth shooting for. Don't tell me it's not an admirable goal. Now, I may or may not be a man of integrity, and you might have your own opinions on the matter, considering everything, but I can tell ya, you bust your butt one hundred sixty one hundred seventy hours hocking sloops, and you'll be chasing some skirt too. A man's got to have some kind of release, you know? Anyway, who says one-woman-one-man is the law of the land?
 Yeah, if you'll just let me – Yeah, if you'll let me talk, I'll open the whole can of worms right into your lap. Just…just hold on. Hold on. You have to understand, everything was fine and dandy until just an hour ago. And I guess that's where you bumbled in. Just hold on.
 So, release. Over the past few years, I've developed quite a hankering for good ole immoral brandy. Just let me finish. I'll tell ya, just this morning, I rubbed my eyes and tousled my hair, and did what I've become accustomed to: I poured myself a stiff one, you know, shaved (no shower), threw on some smoky pair of khakis I wore the day before yesterday, and a frayed Oxford I bought in 1989, and my loafers with white tube socks, and I split before the wifie-poo could kick the sandman out of her head. These days I've been heading down to Snoop's to line up to the trough with the yachtsies for blueberry cakes. All us sloop-hockers in greater Annapolis come. Well, not all. Nobody would ever invite that bastard Everton Skillton, or his brie-monkey-daughter Ma-de-laine who talks to ya in some kind of Canadian French even if you have no idea why the

fuck she even tries. But pretty much everybody else was there.

As usual, Sam ordered my cakes ten minutes before I got there – I'm always ten minutes late – and when I walk in the door, the curls of blueberry steam are just beginning to lick the ceiling tiles, and the whole joint smells of syrup and confectionary sugar. I'm in heaven. I do, by the way, think it's a shame about my boozing, and so does Sam, and Frank, but yacthsies don't talk about your life – they don't even talk about their lives – and this morning wasn't an exception. It's yachts, yachts, yachts, yachts, yachts, yachts, yachts. Which for the most part is fine with me, see. It just gets olllllllllllld sometimes. I'm talking. I'm talking.

I have to admit, sometimes I want to just skip breakfast altogether, sidestep all the so-called shoptalk, and just get to business. I have to admit, I'm compelled by the insider gossip about who's buying what and who's selling what and who's not doing a damn thing. It's like I'm this little icy moon, and Snoop's and the boys are Jupiter, and I don't have a choice in the matter. Usually though, the only day of the week that I miss out on Snoop's is Sundays, cause those're the days we all go to St. Luke's Presby and get free donuts and coco after the service. I know, I know. But we do it since we can eat much as we want – and we take the as-much-as-you-want part serious. Pastor and all the pole-up-their-asses-church mice are starting to get POed at us for eating five or six donuts apiece, but that's their problem. As if it's our fault they got to resort to gimmicks to get anybody to pay their weekly respects. My soul feels fine.

I'm getting to it. So, this morning at Snoop's, Bill and Hendricks started ribbing me about the ladies, which I have to say – no disrespect to them – I didn't much appreciate. Hendricks is always trying to get the upper hand with his mouth, since he knows too well his wallet is a mute. He started saying I cut more trim with other people's wives than most men cut with their own. Now this – no offense – sounds like a compliment in some circles, but with these fellows it was backhanded. Yeah, that's right. Buster, despite all appearances, the yachtsies are good family men, and they take pride in that, and most of them have rug-rats, and mortgages, and a burgundy Ford Taurus in the driveway next to the peonies and the dwarf nandina. Yeah, whatever. So what Hendricks said was supposed to make me look like an immature, lecherous, black-sheep – which I plainly and happily am – and then Bill added insult to injury with his twitchy little pimp mustache and Bermuda prints. "Stan, ever wonder what your wife's doing while you're out running about?" He just oooooooooozed.

Now that bit wasn't worth its weight in gold, or salt, or whatever in the hell. What Bill and Hendricks didn't know and what I sure wasn't about to tell them was that my wife and I have an understanding that allows me to be the black sheep without being the black sheep, if you get my gist. Everything is fine and dandy with her: we have what some people might call an enlightened relationship. I mean, I notice the missing money, but aside from that... Yeah, she wanted the joint checking. This is why I was trying to tell you it wasn't personal. I mean, she is your wife, but...yeah, join the club. That's what I'm trying to tell you...

Right, and it was seven fifteen already, and I had to part ways with the world of men different type of situation altogether. Good golly, Nancy's been with me for nearly three years, I suppose. We have the mornings. This particular morning she greeted me with the regular regal treatment, scratching my shoulders, and murmuring in my ear, and kicking her feet side to side like she had a hopper down her drawers. "Have I got news for you," she said. This is how she always greeted me, as if she had something so urgent to tell me that she can't possibly pause for a "hello," or a "hi," or a "hey." She's the type of woman to just laze into things, and muck around in it like a warthog in a radish patch. I hate to throw anybody into a pigeonhole, but Nancy's the coffee and cigarette type, although she doesn't smoke and only has a cup a day. Or maybe she's what you would call BoHo. At any rate, she smells of cabbage constantly, which might give her the chronic self-esteem issues she grapples with. Anyway, she's short and stout with this trollish German look to her. Put simply, she's not exactly a beauty, and she knows it. Which makes you think: why in God's name did I get involved with an ugly troll woman who smells of vegetables? This is the great affair? Right, she was *there*.

But I'm telling you, this hausfrau's got a wit.

"Let me guess," I said.

"Guess," she said.

"You croaked in your sleep and woke up in the body of a cricket," I said. "No."

"What was it then?" I asked. We were always talking about her dream-life, which I guess says something about our state of affairs. Escapism, sure.

"I was dreaming that you and I went on our honeymoon and–"

"We're going on our honeymoon," I said.

"Right, and we were lying in bed after sex. We were naked," she said, closing the door behind her and holding the knob behind her back.

"Right," I said.

"And you said to me, 'Nancy, have you ever read *Red and Black* by Stendhal?' And I laughed, because it was so ridiculous. Like something some old lady would ask me in the crafts aisle, and I said, 'Why, does it turn you on?' And you said, 'No, I just was wondering.' And that was it." At this point, she was swiveling on the doorknob like a marionette.

"That was all?" I asked.

"That was all I remember," she said.

"That is the most boring dream I've ever heard of," I said. "That was our honeymoon? Forget it. It's off."

"No, they were all there," she said. I'll explain. With that she snapped the doorknob from her hand and stretched her arms over her head and yawned. She asked me if I wanted anything to drink, and I said I wanted brandy, and she poured me some in a tall Coca-Cola glass. Out of the four of them, I was most concerned with Nancy. She was still young, and she seemed more distracted recently, as if she was lost in reflection, and as far as this set-up was concerned, reflection meant bad.

I asked her: "So, are you saying you think life with us is going to be boring?"

"Oh no. Oh honey – I don't think that," she said. She flopped down on her ratty shit-brown sofa and pulled an afghan over her feet. "No, if anything, I've just been working too much. Fiction all day long, and you know, whenever I shelve in the fiction section, some old lady comes up to me and asks what I think of this book, or that book. I usually tell them I like the author, you know? Even if I don't know anything about them. But sometimes I just tell them the truth. I don't know why I lie to some of them."

"You like pleasing people," I told her. "And you make a mountain out of a mole-hill."

"It's true," she said. "I hate seeing these old ladies go home disappointed."

"Even if they find out later that Sten-whatever-his-name-is is a long-winded bore?"

"Yeah, but they don't. They listen to my opinion, and that's how they read the book," she said. "They look for the good in it. Most of them at least."

No. Lookit, Nancy was just the first in Annapolis. When we first moved to Maryland six years ago, it was just Karen and I, and we were content. Coming from Belmont – the Great Lakes area – we always found more to do around here, you know? But after a couple of years, I started to get itchy. I met Nancy when I was in the grocery store buying some tea for Karen. Karen has allergies, and she thinks herbal teas help, so there I was buying Bellwort Brew or something of the sort when Nancy came up to me and said that she'd seen my signs up near the city dock, and that she thought boats were beautiful (since then she's learned that however much she doesn't care about books, that's twice as much as I don't care about boats), and I told her they were, and I gave her my card. The next day I was over at her apartment doing all kinds of unmentionables. Needless to say, this wasn't expected. Yeah, it ran hot and heavy for a year. She was only twenty-one then. Finishing up at St. John's. I was only her second lover ever, so I had the privilege factor. She's my vulnerable little girl.

Right. It is interesting. I hope this gives you some understanding. That's right. When Karen found out about Nancy (I wasn't about to tell her), she was plenty angry for a day or two, storming about, making me sleep in the hall. Karen's an independent type though, and a thinker of sorts, and she's ultimately given to accepting things for the way they are. This is why it was so difficult when she found out that we couldn't... Yeah, no kids at all. It broke her heart. She pulled me aside – never in a million will I forget it – and she said, "Stan, I love you with all my heart." She said: "I do have unconditional love for you for some reason, and I have to be understanding and let you do what you need to do. Otherwise you'd resent me, and this would be a lost cause." She's really an amazing woman. She didn't gasp and whimper. No tears. Karen simply shook her head in self-doubt, blaming herself, pointing the finger at her own dowdiness and lack of enthusiasm. "From now on," she said. "I want you to do whatever you want. You have your little dates. You do what ever you need to do. That's unconditional love, right? I'll still love you. Just don't leave me in the process. Just don't leave me alone." That was three years ago.

I'm sure deep down the whole agreement must be hell for her. What an effort of restraint! I respect the hell out of her. Yeah. I see. You must think I'm this callous woman baiting misogynist, who doesn't care about his own wife. But it's not true. Well, it's true in a way, but I still have a heart. Nancy cares about me still, through some Godly effort. What happened is she agreed – yes agreed – that her, Nancy, and your wife and I would make a good family together. Especially considering our inability... Now hold on. Yeah, we can't. Never been able to... Anyway, it took some convincing to get Nancy especially to go for it, but finally everyone agreed that today would be the day. This pastor that we know would unofficially marry all of us, and we'd live happily ever after. But as you know... Okay, just hold your horses there, cowboy. I'm getting there. Watch it, buster.

So that was Nancy. Sensitive, hardworking, conscientious, dreamy, loving, romantic, and not a little bit wispy. She would make croissants for me, and serve fresh fruit and tea. I'd get there around seven and we'd usually have until nine-thirty when she had to get to work. We'd make love (she liked slow romantic missionary-style), and then talk in the way people talk early in the morning, respectful, thoughtful, purposeful. We'd talk about what we had on the plate for the rest of the day. She'd tell me about her friends, and her parents and brothers, and her cartooning classes, and what she made for herself last night for dinner.

Carla was a whole different ball game altogether, boy. See, I met this woman on a sale. About a year ago, I got a Howdy Doody from her husband Gill, who's a big-deal corporate lawyer in D.C. He wanted to purchase a thirty-foot Tartan sloop, and at the time I didn't have one on the listings, so I was off on my search. This wasn't unusual. I'm always getting customers scouring the harbors from county to county, looking for their customized boat, whatever it may be. I finally found a Tartan for sale all the way out in Cambridge, but he was more than willing to go track it down with me. So I drove up to his mansion outside of town (long-ass commute for him) and he strutted towards me with Carla around his arm, wide smile, his hair slicked back and tie just so, like he owned the damn town. When I started up my Skylark, their leather and potpourri stink filled the car.

As I drove them over there, I told them about the Tartan, or as much as I could discern from the listing and a ten-minute phone call to the owner. Usually on a first go I'll ask a lot of questions to test the knowledge of my clients, ask about how they're going to finance this purchase, see what they are really looking for, dive into a deeper understanding of their motives for wanting a yacht. When you're in yacht sales, you get a lot of people who say they want a thirty-footer, right, and they'll jump up and up and up until they land at a sixty or seventy-foot boat. Not these folks though. Lookit, right away I could tell they – no, he – knew what they wanted, and why. Gill was a sort of mundane aficionado – casually dropping hints about this and that, but not in an obvious self-conscious I'm-going-to-show-you-what-I-know manner. The guy knew his tits from his tats; it was part of his blood. Which I found out it was: Gill was old – I mean ancestors from the Mayflower old – New England money who came down to the Mid-Atlantic to escape the insiders claustrophobia, and Carla was just his little fuck-toy to do with what he pleased.

So after a half-hour's bull, everything's quiet. We're driving down Route Sixty-One and I see Gill with his head back on the seat coughing and Carla leaning away from him with a wince, as if she didn't give two shits if he was coughing up his lungs or not, and I was sure she'd rather be just about anywhere else. Suddenly their image, their mansion, their lives, everything about them seemed to be a flimsy front. Carla was trying to tell me something. I looked in the rearview, and Carla was looking right at me. Her eyes weren't looking through me to our destination, but right at me, piercing wormholes in my brain. I asked her if he was okay, and she said he was. He coughed again and groaned – which I thought was a ploy to loosen me for some guilt bargaining – and she whispered that he hasn't been feeling well for a while. "I don't know why we're out here," she said. I tried to ask him if he wanted me to stop and get him a drink of water, but she said he just needed to sit quietly, that he had a headache. But this woman was still giving me a run over. She leaned up to the front seat and said, "Things have been tough with us these days." Yes, believe me. I was thinking along the same lines. I mean, what was I supposed to do? I had to take advantage of the situation.

Well, they ended up buying the Tartan – a sort of pick-me-up for hubby – and what do you know, the little lady wanted to meet up with me to sign the papers. He hacked and coughed and gave her full contractual leeway. I said ta-ta, and he limped up the long walk. So fifteen minutes later, we're sitting there at the restaurant and I'm touching on all the finer points of the purchase, and she's nodding and initialing, and she scoots a little closer to where I'm sitting, and her shoe is touching my shoe, and she scoots a little closer, and her sleeve is touching my sleeve, and she scoots a little closer, and I can smell what she ate for breakfast. We got some soft Haggard on the sound system. I take a drink of water; she takes a drink of water. I can tell something's going on, and I'm nervous. She looks at my wedding ring and says, "Is that a joke or what?" I laugh, because what else am I supposed to do with this girlie? I say "You've got some spirit in you, huh?" And she says: "I'd like to have something in me other than just spirit."

On the heated rush to the hotel, she gives me the run-down. Born and raised in Vermont, home of the no-nonsense. She was the only girl in her high school to have two boys at the same time, and she was proud of it. She went to college in Ohio, but dropped out after a year and a half – temptations. She got a job as a secretary for a construction company in Cleveland, and fell in love with the manly atmospherics. You know, all the sweat and grunting. Sure. The men would come in twice a week to see if their paycheck came in, just to see Carla. She moonlighted as some kind of exotic dancer – for the bucks at first, she said – later to escape. Yeah, to tell you the truth,

I don't believe it, but that's what she said. She went through a string of construction worker boyfriends, but they became a blur after a spell, and she wanted a different type of man altogether. That's when Gill came along – litigation suit against another construction company. When they first met, he was on top of his game, she said. He was energetic and ambitious and filled with sex and sensuality, but as time wore on, the lawyer life took its toll. "We were doing it once a night for the first year of our marriage, and then it just fell off to three times a week. Then twice. Recently just once a month, if I'm lucky. I guess he got bored," she said. "I don't know. Being a lawyer would do that to me too. But I'm sorry, I need somebody to pay attention to me. It's a cliché, I know, but he's fucking his secretary."

Yeah, wow. Now, Carla takes some of the wind out of my sails to tell you the truth, because here's the thing I want to tell you: what drives me to all this philandering is that I basically have no respect for these women. Isn't that the way it goes? Yeah, I know. I can't help it, man. But I'm a guy who realizes his dependency upon women (a weakness in my book). I realize that I need them around to make me feel like I got all my horses running. You know what I mean? I'm not into blow-up dolls and plastic lips, porno and all that jazz; I need the real deal. And with some of them like Carla, I actually enjoy what they have to say. But in my opinion, Carla is meant to be a man – which is maybe why I enjoy her company.

So anyway, Carla and I developed this lunchy type relationship. Once a week, sometimes twice, I'd meet her at the Pine Motel in Arnold, and we'd have our time, and then we'd go out for lunch, and then go back to the room. It all made sense. Carla had this winsome, honest personality that was perfect with chicken clubs. As our time together progressed, I could see that heavy load lighten, and she rarely mentioned her husband at all. Our relationship became a sort of erotic testing ground for our other flings – she had something going on with Grady Bolton down at the DMV (Vermonter: she was getting in touch with her roots), and she wanted to explore.

Carla bolstered my opinion that I wanted to be with all the women in my life all the time, or at least as much of the time as possible. She got me to believe that I did want a sort of simultaneous universe. A harem, man. No, I'm not Mormon. When I told her my idea, she laughed at first. She said she would have a hard time leaving Gill with his sacks of dough and yachts and fancy cars, but later she was drawn to me, and to this idea of a community of people all loving me (and each other if necessary).

"Who's talking about you leaving him?" I said.

"Isn't that what you mean now?" she said.

"No, that's not what I mean at all," I said. "If you get married to me, you don't have to leave him. It's not – it won't be an official marriage. It'll be a living arrangement."

I won't bore you. We talked about the ins and outs, and then she said: "I don't know. He does need me. He does rely upon me. He's pretty pathetic, you know."

"Yeah, well…"

"But I can't build something on weak ground," she said. She put her hand on my knee and mussed my hair. It didn't take a whole lot of convincing.

I met your wife at – where else – the yacht club. I know, I know. But what else is there for someone to do during the day in Annapolis? So she was there, sitting at a corner table in the yacht club sipping coffee. It was late in the evening, and the sun hit her just so. She lit up from within like some expensive new-age lamp. That particular day I was in a hurry, since I was meeting Harvey Kline and the sellers, the Timmermans. But even at first glance, I entered her into my mental repository, see.

Now Harvey made me work, boy, and I was falling into dangerous territory. Emotionally, he sidled up to me and patted me on the back and said everything was going to be fine, even though I was starting to question my own abilities to sell – I had a bit of a dry spell at the time. "Let's just have fun with it," he'd say, and we'd race all over Anne Arundel and Calvert County looking at boats – a forty-seven-foot Gulfstar Sailmaster, a forty-two-foot Catalina, a fifty-five-foot Roberts Steel Ketch. It was almost as if he didn't care if he bought a boat or didn't buy a boat, he just wanted to see as many of the suckers as he could. Now, back when I lived in Michigan, I used to be naïve and take my customers out on the lake and feed them at the yacht club afterwards, but I learned my lesson.

When I first started, I tried to please the buyer no matter what. Now I don't take anybody out on a yacht unless I have the deposit in my hand. There's a reason banks run from yacht loans.

Anyway, that particular day at the yacht club, Harvey and the Timmermans seemed to be on good terms. His offer was close enough to the asking price that it was a ball game. Harvey started off the proceedings by blowing sunshine up the Timmermans' asses. "You have to love the details," he said. "You guys must have put years renovating the beauty." Mr. Timmerman told him about the weeks spent on the leather interior, the Corian countertops, the Italian lighting, the teak and mahogany bulkheads. "It sure is a beauty there," Harvey said. "Your hard work is going to pay off in spades."

Despite the amiable surface, I was a mess worrying about getting chiseled on the deal. I hadn't sold a boat in a month, and I had bills to pay, mouths to feed. I could see Harvey pleasantly backing out of this deal, stringing me along for another week or two. I just wanted to get pen to paper before it was winter and half the boats would be in storage – you never sell shit then. But the biggest danger was the fact that I'd become friendly with Harvey, and I could feel my guard slipping. As Harvey was reading the fine print, my mind kept fading into a negative sphere. I kept thinking how the only reason Harvey was considering buying this boat was to get more skirt. It's no secret men buy their boats for women, name them after women, and refer to them as women. Harvey didn't seem like a pure womanizer, but the sexual glint in his eye when he talked about the yacht was unmistakable. Then I retreated farther from the contractual chatter, again thinking how nice it would be to be a housedaddy, watch my wives support me, send my progeny to chef school. I just want children, man.

When it was all said and done, Harvey signed on the dotted line. The Timmermans whooped and bought a bottle of the finest bubbly, and we leaned back and savored the moment. Then the moment was finis. Harvey and the Timmermans shook my hand and left in a whirl, and I sat alone at the table with a view of Jan. Now, I have to say it's never been difficult to meet a woman in a yacht club. Any time a lady's alone in a yacht club, she's usually thinking with her matrimonial drive – looking for some rich doctor to sweep her off her feet.

With Jan it was different. You know. I fell in love with her intensity. She came up to me that day as I sat at that table by my lonesome, feeling my typical mix of post-sale elation and release, and she sat down across from me without saying a word. Honestly, she just stared at me, and then slowly bent her neck and unclasped her purse, and withdrew a piece of yellow paper. She handed me the paper, and I read it without saying a word. It was a party invitation, to a dance party at some guy's house. I carefully folded the invitation on the table, and released it so the flaps of the paper sprang upwards.

"Are you trying to tell me something?" I asked.

"Yeah, I'm trying to tell you that you're invited to this thing if you want to go. Not that you're special or anything." She lifted my empty champagne glass to her mouth, and overturned it so that several drops of champagne dribbled onto her tongue.

"Of course not," I said. She lightly replaced the champagne glass where it sat before, exactly matching the circle of the glass to the circle of the glass sweat on the table.

"The guy who's holding the party was just walking around city dock handing them out. I guess it's going to be a big deal," she said.

"Either that or he's desperate for friends," I said.

"You're probably right," she said. "Yet, I find myself curiously drawn to the idea of being invited to crash a party. I rarely get the opportunity to go to a party anymore. You?"

"No," I said. Yeah, I know.

So we went. I don't know what Jan told you, but it was simply one of the greatest evenings of my life. See, the party was packed with interesting, lively people. I felt like I was suddenly part of some new insiders' circle, and that I lucked upon all of this through my chance meeting with Jan. We danced. We drank too much, and as I already told you, we…consummated our relationship. Okay, okay. I'll tell you. Well, I love her sense of fashion. I love her movement, how she retained her sexuality… I'm just jealous. She's quite a catch. No, she wasn't. No, she was never disparaging of you.

I guess what you don't know is that every Friday night we began meeting. We would go out dancing most of the time, dancing until three in the morning and leaving reeking of smoke and sweat, and going our separate ways before we collapsed. Sometimes we'd meet at a hotel, and then go out to dinner. To be honest, she never mentioned you. Hey, I'm just telling you. I knew she was married. Yes, but I didn't know to whom, and I didn't really want to know. It was enough just to be with her when I could be with her.

And today? Well, we met over two years ago. She said she was ready and willing for anything. She trusted me. She wanted in. So who was I to say no? She didn't mind the others. As long as she could have her time with me when need be, she would be content. But then, you know the rest. Hey, I didn't force your hand on that. We all live with our mistakes. Mine wasn't a mistake though, that's what I'm saying. Hell no. I'm not living that way. Adjust yourself. I'm not changing.

Put it away now. Okay. Okay. I know all of this sounds odd to you. I don't blame you. I don't. This is me. Right, I know. Just try to…understand. It's right there in the Old Testament. All those guys had wives galore. It's not unusual. Hold on. Just see it through my eyes, and try to understand. Man to man, I told you the truth. I swear, it wasn't about you at all.

THE RATIONALIST

I desire to be taken seriously. As evidence, my amorous goal: to acquire a lover of good standing who firmly believes in the dictum that men and women are *not* created equal. To wit: that men are substantially the superior sex, who shall design and dictate the larger whims of the weaker. I am a man of compassion. I seek the ultimate goal of a woman's liberation through her awareness of her own – albeit inferior – social position and standing. Truly, by recognizing one's social position and standing, one's floodgates of realization are swung widely open. For I do believe women are categorically as entitled to a modicum of liberty as men.

However, the difficulty of my unusual endeavor is apparently the somber fact that I am clearly in the minority in this worldview, which makes the prospect of finding such a woman distinctly slight. As one might suspect, I have found of yet only the slimmest success in this grand project – this despite its seven-year tenure. I withdraw once or twice a week to the same coffee bar on the edge of town, where I proceed to sit by the entrance and attempt conversation (quite brazenly, I might add) with various samples of the female species. Occasionally I will scout a potentially rewarding position at a local bar, or mall, or at the park by the lake. Location, location, location. Yet, this enterprise is not without its foibles and necessary drawbacks – namely out-right rejection – and at times, I have wavered in my dedication to such a goal. Yet, I must fight the good fight, so to speak. I must endure.

My wife, Linda, lambastes me for accusustomarily rousing between the hours of 11:30 and 11:59 in the morning, however, I maintain that a critic by necessity needn't operate on the schedule of a government drone. I need my brain sleep, as she needs her beauty sleep. The help arrives at seven, as Linda is promptly departing for her position in the city, and remains until my awaking. At times, I must be roused from my scrumptious slumber, since my six-year-old

RANTS AND RAVES

daughter Emily has needs or questions of which I am the primary target. This morning she – Emily – is happily reclining at the kitchen table, readying herself for her noontime meal, when I stride into said room prepared for my morning breakfast.

"Goddddd. Daaaaaaaaaad," she wails. The help is even startled.

"Esmerelda?" The help looks curious.

"No, me llamo María."

"Oh, sí. Yes," I translate. I think perhaps Maria herself has misplaced the meaning to the Spanish affirmative.

"Could you please help my daughter? Anything she may desire." The help nods, and she yammers and blabbers in her native tongue, as the female species is wont to do. I'm in the middle of my morning ritual, not to be disturbed by meaningless drivel. I stride confidently to the notepad on the counter, underneath my treasured bulletin board. On said counter is a note from Linda. The note reads:

Dear Richard,

I may not be back from work until 7:30 this evening. Please fix dinner for Emily. Use the leftover chicken, macaroni, and you can make a salad.

Steps:
1. *Remove chicken from refrigerator (Hint: it's not the beef).*
2. *Microwave chicken. The microwave is the box with the knobs.*
3. *Take knife out of drawer.*
4. *Chop the chicken into bite-sized chunks and feed to Emily if necessary.*
5. *Microwave macaroni.*
6. *Macaroni is a pasta dish. We had it yesterday.*
7. *Ditto #2, save the chopping.*
8. *Wash lettuce. Wash carrots. Wash tomatoes. I assume you know what these vegetables are.*
9. *Slice into a bowl and top with salad dressing.*
10. *Please refrain from watching inane teenage sex movies all the livelong day.*

Love,
Your wife.

Aside from the highly insulting and patronizing manner in which my "soul mate" worded her desires, I immediately question her esteem for my profession (a certain sore point in our marriage). As I am a film critic for *The Post-Times*, my profession calls me to be aware of major and minor cinematic trends, and industry tidbits of the most minuscule nature. My weekdays usually consist of DVD and/or video watching, a tremendous amount of note taking, and a marginal amount of writing (I usually write two reviews a week). Linda, however, is at times under the impression that my film watching ("habit," as she calls it) is interfering with my parental duties. I have gently reminded her on many occasions that this so-called "habit" funds us with a sizable income, perhaps not equivalent, or indeed competitive with her fancy-pants corporate attorney dough, but nevertheless enough to at least pay for the mortgage and Emily's tuition. Habitually, Linda rebuts this response to her argument by waving me off, gesticulating as would a common orangutan, or uttering the casual "puleeeeeeeease, Richard." I am the woman; she is the man.

Moreover, I am suddenly keenly aware that this note has signaled a new and terrifying shift in her mental processes. Now she considers *me* part of the help! I won't have it. I unhinge the bulletin board from the wall, wedge it under my arm, prepare and rapidly consume my morning brew (along with a delicious gourmet tomato-basil bagel with light honey-nut cream-cheese), and I am, as they say "outta there," as I briskly tell the help that I'll be back later in the afternoon, "mucho later," I translate.

"Wait, Mr. Glinko," I hear someone say. Nope. That abode is not my responsibility after the outside portal has closed. I quickly hop in Willa, my sky-blue Jaguar, and am off. I see flabby arms flailing down the art deco tiling. Those tiles are quite lovely, I think. At least Linda has a sense of décor.

I drive approximately 1/10 of a mile and park at the large warehouse-style strip mall, where one might find an office store, a glorified convenience store, a bookstore, a coffee shop: the accoutrements of suburbia. Today I am headed to the coffee shop, carrying my bulletin board (as one must on such occasions), to dispel my feelings of inadequacy, aggravation, and displeasure by potentially (with all the will I can muster) developing a fling with said desired and available woman. On a note of urban planning, American neighborhoods would be vastly more entertaining – not to mention healthy – if they cultivated well-stocked brothels within the inner sanctum of suburbia, especially so to relieve the menfolk of their disastrous urges. I simply refuse to risk life and limb to patronize the whorehouses of downtown Baltimore, of all places; I shall wait patiently for the call girls to approach *me* on their (albeit infrequent) house calls in cozy Catonsville.

At any rate, I enter the halls of commerce as the sweet aroma of air-conditioned cappuccino wafts hither and thither, many a ravenous diner engorge themselves on delicate pastried ambrosia. I find my normal place of respite in the general vicinity of the transition zone between the coffee-bar and the entrance proper, whereby I recline hands behind head, feet propped on the chair adjacent to mine, scanning the store for potential mates. I work myself up to a sort of "esprit cavalier" by perusing my favorite quotes on my bulletin board (in order of preference):

1. *He that hath wife and children hath given hostages to fortune; for they are impediments to great enterprises; either of virtue or mischief.* – Francis Bacon.
2. *Nature has given hearts to bulls, hoofs to horses, swiftness to hares, the power of swimming to fishes, of flying to birds, understanding to men. She had nothing more for women save beauty. Beauty is proof against spears and shields. She who is beautiful is more formidable than fire and iron.* – Anacreon
3. *What a woman says to her ardent lover should be written in wind and running water.* – Catullus.
4. *Nothing enchants the soul so much as young women. They alone are the cause of evil, and there is no other.* – Bharitihari.

Oh, there are so many wonderful nuggets! Yet these particular quotes are not merely for the purpose of illustration, but of potential and delicious fornication. They are a litmus test: for any lover of mine will agree with at least one quote among the pickings. It is a tried and true technique (although, as of yet, as I said, quite unsuccessful).

As I am sitting in the coffee bar awaiting my Venus, who should walk into the room but Mina, an old college girlfriend. She is with a tall gentleman wearing a purple Armani suit, who leads her to the coffee bar, speaking all the while in a clipped New York accent that my Mina, of course, was formerly never in possession of in the least. Oh, in those golden days, there were so many women at my disposal, since my tastes had not yet been cultivated to their currently high level. Seemingly in those days, I was a magnet for women of all sorts – punk rockers, biker-chicks, prima donnas, cuddly Japs, hopeful lesbians, sorority bimbos, and opportunists of every stripe. Then, upon graduation, I was introduced to Linda by my dear parents – who subsequently informed me that she was of the moneyed class. Our quasi-parasitic relationship was thus established; she provided while I subsisted, and for years I didn't lift a happy finger. All of which is not to say Linda failed to instruct me on the ways of a marriage – she taught me how to proffer myself for the sake of American comfort. Linda instructed me quite well in how to operate as a private (though unpaid) sperm bank, how to speak in hushed tones.

Fortunately, Mina and mate scurry to their respective restrooms, and zip back out undetected. Ah, the unpaid pit stop: a staple of American life, of which I am quite familiar. Although I revel in the avoided confrontation, and/or awkward exchange, I applaud Mina and mate for their apparent parasitic subversion of said coffee bar.

Temporarily I decide to abandon my quest, to call Emily. I am hiding – just in case Mina returns. For several reasons, I actually feel pangs of guilt wash over me (though certainly, it is a gentle wash). Emily answers the phone upon its third consecutive ring.

"Em?" I declare.

"Daddy?"

"Yes, honey. Is the assistance still tending to your every need?"

"Who?"

"The help. Is she still present? Is she with you?"

"She is leaving right now, Daddy. She has to go home." My daughter is very matter of fact about these things. Kids.

"I will be home in a bit, okay? Can you be okay by yourself?" Of course she will answer in the affirmative. What should I expect? I loathe the belittling voice I use with my daughter, yet it is the one that I am expected to maintain. She will be fine all by herself. Many psychologists claim that by six a child is developmentally almost a teenager. She can certainly open the refrigerator, and find her way to the commode. She won't drown unless she decides to act an imbecile, and shower or bathe, or something of this absurd nature. I am suddenly overwhelmed by feelings of pride over the independence of my big girl.

"Daddy is doing a very important errand."

"Okay. I'm a monkey," she declares, and starts making monkey noises. "Ooooooooooooooo. Ooooooooooo. Ooooooo. Naaaaaaaa. Naaaaaaaaa. Naaaaaaaa."

"Yes, you are, honey. I will be back home to feed you your bananas soon. Don't burn anything or chop the chairs up with an axe. Okay?"

"Ooooooooooooo. Ooooooooooo. Ooooooooooo." My wife overestimates me at every turn in regards to my paternal qualities and abilities, and this is yet another reason to casually dismiss these small duties on a whim.

Woman number one is tall, lanky, and slightly awkward in gait (reminding me immediately of a gazelle), dressed in a limber set of black slightly gothic shorts (pockets stitched close to the hip) and a ragged blue ribbed tank-top, with the acronym "W.A.R." emblazoned in yellow across the front. She appears to be a woman of unconventional tastes and beliefs – a perfect first candidate. I watch her every muscular gesticulation as she laces her way past an older woman pushing her grandson, two high school boys in knit caps, and a coffee shop wench clinking and clanking her merry way to the sink encumbered with a tray of soiled dishes. As Gazelle orders her regular coffee, and readies herself for the transfer to a table on the far side of the coffee establishment, I firmly place myself in her route to avoid the overly complicated "hard sell approach." With a sigh, I purposefully-accidentally bump her, slightly jostling her coffee, enough to dribble a spoonful onto the parquet flooring. Her response to this is a passing shrug, barely noticing the cause of said disruption (me); she knows this drill well. Yet, I surprise the little antelope – as she begins her escape route into the thickets of the coffee bar, I tap her just above the right collarbone and cough gently, the way women truly desire to be interrupted as they go about their activities during the day.

"Excuse me, miss," I say. I decide my strategy will consist of an attempt to appear thoughtful-yet-sensitive, while at the same time remaining energetic and culturally knowledgeable about the arts (I'm sure "W.A.R." stands for some artist collaborative, or far-left guerilla political action group); I pensively scratch my three-day-old-beard-in-the-making, and bend towards the darling gazelle with a gesture of overly-elaborate (bordering on Japanese), and slightly self-conscious curtsy. Unfortunately she whips around and gazes at me blankly, as if I were a stalker or a crippled Bible-salesman sloughing outside BWI with my mustard stains and my blind dog, Beefcake.

"I couldn't help but notice that I may have, um, jostled your coffee."

"So," she shrugs. "Forget about it." She turns again to beat her retreat to the well-lit netherworld of the establishment.

"Please, allow me to purchase you another beverage," I assert.

"I said forget it," she responds. Then the fiery antelope does, in fact, escape my grasp, leaving me standing in the hub of a coffee bar in my sweat pants and crinkled t-shirt, with my metaphorical – excuse the language – genitalia in hand. Well, I can hardly leave this as is. I approach her table, where she ever so quickly buries her nose in a volume of *The Films of Frank Capra*. You must understand, as keen as I am upon finding a lady-friend who may be aligned with my sexual politics and overall worldview, my cinematic tastes are by far more vital to my reputation as a critic and intellectual. I feel suddenly nauseous.

"Capra?" I exclaim.

"Yeah," she retorts, without lifting her nose from said volume.

"Get a fucking job, dirtbag."

This inspires a great long-winded speech, in which I unleash with furious dynamism a tirade against the ills of sentimentalist cinema (especially in the guise of the classic Hollywood aesthetic). If she thinks of me as a vagrant with a taste for now obscure European cinema of the early 60s, so be it. I will not have this ignorant youth decontaminate the environs of this fine coffee establishment with her drivel about Mr. Capra's value as a so-called filmmaker. I conclude my diatribe with the following statement: "You soft-hearted liberals would have every film ruined by syrupy shots of cute dogs and cooing babies. Don't you know that Capra inspired Spielberg! Of all the directors, you go for the bottom of the barrel? Shame on you! Shame!"

"Who really cares, man? I was looking for–"

"Intelligent people do care, miss. I could list a thousand directors more interesting than Frank Capra, of all people."

Gazelle simply shrugs (apparently her favorite non-verbal expression-cum-tic) and responds: "Whatever you're selling…I'm not interested."

"Selling? I'm not…" I feel faint. At this point I try to show her my quotes, but she laughs in my face. Shamed, I stumble back and away from this woman.

Selling? Selling? Of all the disgraceful rejections and offences, this is clearly one of the lowest. My entire existence has been to counter the appearance and or/affectations of commerce (aside from my suave maneuvers with the weaker sex). Thus I decide to move my shop to friendlier confines – a real bar, where the imbibed substances may, in fact, play more in my favor.

As I methodically steer myself away from the coffee bar, and in the direction of the nearest tavern, I cannot help reflecting on the nature of my decision making process. I suppose I am indeed a sort of antiquated rationalist, and yet in addition, I am a sensitive type easily scarred by unfair accusations. At times I fear I am rent between these two warring personality tics, as a steak would be between two rabid, ravenous mongrels. Yet, somewhere along the line, fate has entered into the bargain, leaving my waking consciousness out of the equation altogether. This is not the way it was supposed to be!

When I was a young man, I studied with furious diligence the works of the classical rationalists – Descartes, Spinoza, Leibniz. I was immediately taken by the purity of their collective worldview (although I was, of course, aware of the differences between their philosophies, I was primarily interested in their epistemological resemblances). The true source of knowledge is reason, not the senses; the correct philosophical model is a priori; ego cogito sum. Baruch Spinoza lived out his life grinding lenses, excommunicated from synagogue, loathed by the Dutch Calvinists. All excellent things *are* as difficult as they are. Who knows about God, other than the fact that the infinite substance surely exists? Spinoza in particular led me to the phenomenologists; all consciousness *is* consciousness of itself. Yes. I found maxims to live by – guidance.

Unfortunately, guidance doesn't guarantee contentment. At times I wonder if this logic-driven mindset has not doomed me to a position in which I have become a caricature of myself, a ridiculous fop with an exceedingly outmoded set of logical suppositions. The women I attempt to seduce seemingly view me as an unwarranted mixture of garden-variety sleaze-ball, and circus clown. Yet, the objects of my affection fail to comprehend that the phenomenological side of my character curiously ponders what it must *be like* to exist in the skin and bones of a woman at the cusp of the twenty-first century. I wonder, what is it *really* like? This is precisely the moment when I realize that if I were a woman, I would view myself with the same sort of disgusted ambivalence, as do many of my potential amours. When this realization sets in, the world comes crashing down upon my very head (usually provoking my voyage home). Yet, today I am still filled with the requisite optimism and faith it must take to be successful in any venture of the sexual nature; one cannot go about these things half-heartedly with any hopes of fulfillment. One must choose to forget.

I enter Lew's Bar casually, as if I chose the abode by accident – an often-breathtaking mode of access. Although it is early in the afternoon, the establishment is filled with couples eating lunch together, men playing Keno at the bar proper, and young women huddling en masse near the dance floor while eyeing the male patrons and street passersby through a large bay-window. Two years ago, I decided to proceed along a path of straight and narrow (no alcohol), yet to bag one of these tarts, I think perhaps the appearance of a border-line drunkard is called for: I order a non-alcoholic beer, and lean back to survey the surroundings.

Lew's is a typical lounge in many aspects, except one: it is close to the college, and thus attracts a number of attractive young women, many of whom seemingly move in herds in search of a similar herd of Mr. Rights. The herd positioned by the window is composed of seven women – a redhead, a short brunette, two lanky blonde gazelles, two black beauties, and a birdy woman of unknown ethnic origin (Arab? Portuguese? Polynesian?), and last but not least, a muscular woman wearing a mini-skirt and black t-shirt, who appears to be a year or two older than the others. Needless to say, the last is my primary object of interest. I decide to approach her the moment she breaks away from the herd (presumably to attend to the jukebox or bathroom), as a lion would pounce on a stray and limping wildebeest.

I have a long wait. *The Apartment*: Jack Lemmon lending his apartment to philandering senior executives. If only we still lived in an old boys network where men looked out for each other, where arrangements are made for universal interest. Today, as is the case with our cloven relatives, women drift only out of necessity, and this group is particularly staid and reticent, even though they don't seem to be terribly caught-up in any sort of gripping conversation or debate. They tousle their hair, gaze longingly, smile at one another, and seemingly talk about the weather and the latest soaps – the timeless ritual of female bonding is seemingly independent of thought or ideas, and yet these women are part of the work force! No wonder we're losing ground to Asia! After hours of these sorts of meaningless gestures and slight alterations, the amorphous birdy one and the iron-pumper perform a half-sashay, half-cat-walk strut down the main aisle of the tavern. (They can't even pee separately!) I am about to throw in the towel, when the iron-pumper stops directly in front of me, and waves her amorphous companion to go on without her. She firmly pivots her feet so they point directly at me, cocks her head, and with a grand gesture props her arms akimbo.

"You know," she says with a brazen, almost scolding tone, "if you want to talk to me, talk to me."

"I'm sorry," I say. By this point, I'm on my fourth non-alcoholic beer, feeling the unconstructive effects of alcohol (bloated and weary) with none of the encouraging results (drunkenness). I spin in my bar stool in a counter-position so that I might face her offensive.

"My name is–"

"You don't have to stare," she snaps. "I hope I'm not that scary." Despite her muscle tone, she has a jilted woman-next-door quality. One might presume she was a solid A/B student, who joined the speech team in college, and studied international affairs abroad in Paraguay (or some out-of-the-way-but-unique locale, developing a blatant cynicism and streetwise attitude). She reaches into her pocket and withdraws her wedding band; casually she slips it onto her ring finger. I decide this might not be the most opportune time to unleash the bulletin board.

"No, no. Don't be offended. I was simply looking about, you know."

"Right. You don't have to be patronizing. You don't have to play dumb. I'm not an idiot. I can see that you were staring directly at me. I'm not that drunk. But you know what?"

At this juncture I prepare myself for the worst possible scenario – a thrown drink, a kick in the shins, a slap across the face. I've experienced it all. Instead she withdraws a wallet from her purse, opens it, flashing a badge.

"Sir, if you glance my way one more time, I will be forced to apprehend you."

"On what charges? Sitting in a bar?" Did she know about Emily playing monkey at home (and hopefully still refraining from bobbing her sweet little head in and out of the toilet)?

"We can discuss that at the time of arrest. I would really like to have a peaceful moment with my friends. Thank you." She calmly folds her badge back into her purse, and walks casually into the girl's room. Moments after she enters said room, an explosion of laughter emanates from within. "And, I mean, he actually thought it was a policeman's badge!" I heard someone declare. "Moron!" So

now I was the laughing-stock of the bar, the buffoon of the coffee house, and on top of it all…a child abandoner. Our founding fathers established an America that was a land of applied reason and courage, and this is what we have become – irrationality personified, a land where milk and honey are accessible only to those who purchase it outright. I slide a twenty on the sticky bar, and decide to return to my daughter and fatherly pursuits before the gaggle of harpies descends upon me once again.
I shout: "I'll have you know, this is non-alcoholic beer!"

As I drive away from the bar and towards the nestle of woody abodes, where my family resides, I can't help but wonder what the founding fathers think of what they, in part, begat. What would Thomas Jefferson, who had his own legacy of indiscreet affairs, think of male-female relations today? Statistics still show that men (barely) earn more money than their female counterparts, but this is only part of the picture. Statistics show that most women now work. Statistics show that most women like their jobs more than men. Statistics show that women are quickly rising to the top of the ladder, shattering the glass ceiling. My father never had to grapple with such a topsy-turvy world; he provided for the family and returned home to a homecooked meal. He read the paper, and made a drink for himself. Simple. The rational state was still in place pre-*Easy Rider*.

No wonder men live in a state of invariable neurosis. Mine is not so unusual: I want the stability of a wife and family, yet I am sexually repelled by that very stability. Rationality is not simply a peripheral concern for me, but my chosen way of life. Yet, regardless of my physical surroundings, why must I constantly maintain a sex object? What has this garnered for me thus far? I have not had a single affair, or even an indiscretion. A woman could walk into a bar wearing a mini-shirt and a form-hugging shirt of some sort, and develop sexual relations with any married man in the environs. Take Louise Brooks in *Pandora's Box*: women wield power over men. Men must scrap for everything they get; a man can't just get by on looks alone. This is the way of nature – and if Jefferson was right, nature too was deistic and, thus, rational. Yet, on a personal level, nature doesn't *feel* rational.

Several weeks ago, I was at the lake, gazing at a woman fifty yards down the path. The young lady was sunning, but consciously so; she would turn her head every minute or so to see if I was still watching her (I was): a secretary on her lunch break perhaps. This went on for half an hour or so. I would stare; she would sun and then glance my way. I would stare; she would sun and glance my way. Her body language was screaming, "Look at me! Look at me!" In response to this I decided to project the thought "Come to me, come to me." I wanted to see if this woman (or any woman for that matter) would approach me in the way that I might approach them. I wanted to see if I was still desired. After an hour, the woman stood up, brushed herself off, and retreated to her car without a glance. I could not see her form within the tinted hideaway of her car. I thought perhaps she would retrieve some item of necessity from her car (sunglasses, or a hat perhaps), and then at least sidle up to me and squeeze my film critic pecs. Then I heard the car ignite, and the woman drove off. I sat watching the dingy water lap against the lakeside dock for hours.

On the drive home, I chide myself without mercy. I must be a better father; I must be a more devoted husband. Both for my own sanity, and for my family. I must stop chasing floozies. *The Big Heat*: Sergeant Bannion seeking revenge for his wife's murder in the wilds of corrupt law enforcement. I should have such a clear-cut path to redemption. My own destiny is to be with Linda forever, to revel in my own biting purgatory.

I am suddenly weary of rejection, and ready for the easy affirmation of the wife figure – the natural response to a day's worth of nos. This has happened so many times. I am pushed away by others, and I return to the safety of my one woman. This must change, I think. Yet, I cannot seem to help myself. I cannot seem to change despite my own best intentions. After several days of moping around the house, I will return to the hunt, maintaining the vicious cycle.

I drive down the long entrance to our neighborhood, a straight shot past lined pines and spruce. I turn right onto Green Mountain

RANTS AND RAVES

Lane, and left onto Brown Fawn Court. As I glide past the row of boxwoods and rhododendrons, I see my wife's car in the driveway. No. No. Emily. And then there are the changes that you are forced to make; who can control each and every factor? What can one do? Events occur on their own sometimes. What can one do?

Cows

Dear Ruth,

    I am sitting on a tussock above them, as they hump together along the base of the knoll, clustering in the rivulet, and slowly mounting the slope where I recline. I swear to you they are swooning, although I know this is my fancy. I have come again at this late hour simply to watch. In my unnatural state of alertness, they are a comfort to me. I watch their heads lift, their noses slowly admit the humid air, their necks droop to the pasture, their heavy udders sway left to right as they lumber up the slope. The pasture is ripe with dandelion and onion grass; Mrs. Brown's herd must be as sated as Roman Gods.

    Of course not a soul has stirred since I arrived, and her help would never stake a position this close to the herd at this late hour. You must know that even now I am not at all considered an eccentric; no, I suppose it is much worse. I suppose my reputation is still besmirched by the events before you left, yet in a particular way – confined to the lowest nattering, as if to mention it at all would cause both the speaker and listener boils and blisters (this is, in itself, not enough to tarnish the business). I have hired two worthy doctors to do the majority of the so-called "dirty work" (although, as you know, in veterinary medicine it's all dirty work). Since you have gone, they take the general clientele – the chickens, horses, dogs, cats, sheep, goats. I take the cows. Why? I am not sure myself. I suppose it has something to do with their relative inelegance. I know the cows were always my most despised patients, if you will. "Hulking, sweaty, vile beasts," I would always complain. Perhaps I am imposing a sort of atonement on myself. Or perhaps my perspective has truly changed. I'm not sure myself…

    Yet, I must admit I have come to enjoy the company of these beasts. Despite their base qualities, I now see them primarily as placid and gentle, nothing like their brethren. I have made a complete about-face. I now see the bulls as mean-spirited creatures, intent on procreation only, defecating, flatulating, masturbating beasts of purpose. One can hardly walk across a bull's pen without slipping in puddles of semen and feces. At any rate, I thought you should know this. I thought you might hold residual pride for me on this account. I have come a long way.

Love,
Foster

Dear Ruth,

    The Haskells called me this morning, complaining of an adverse cow. As the years pass, this seems more common. I'm not sure if the farmers are becoming lackadaisical on their management, if cows are spooked by the machinery, or if the bulls themselves contain more pent-up vigor, but it seems as if once a week I'm tending a shy one. As I told them, this is usually a matter of feeding. I told the Haskells to put her favorite grasses – maybe dandelion head – in the milking parlor, and calm her with pats and touches. She will go, I said. They said they hadn't tried that with this one – seemed to be too much trouble, yet they called back in an hour: she still refused to budge. You would not believe the mark she had on her flank, almost the length of her body. "This one looks like it napped right on your electric fencing," I said, pointing to the scar. "That kind of trauma would keep her from trusting anybody," I told them. They have to give it a few days and she'll forget, milk her by hand where you can in the meantime. Make the memory seem distant.

    Do you recall the Haskells? You met them at the pancake breakfast at St. John's seven or eight years ago. They are competent dairy farmers, small family affair, doing well, all things considering. Since you left so many city families have moved out here, the likes of the Haskells are becoming scarce. This is why my existence has been so strenuous recently: city families buy two or three cows to go along with their tract mansion, and the next thing you know, you have ten-year-old kids thinking they have a large dog, and mom and dad shrugging their shoulders, saying, "Why don't you see if you can look that up on the internet; I'm not a farmer." I end up racing around from house to house explaining the basics: you have to milk them once a day, don't mix bulls and cows, and don't let calves wean early or mix with adults. A few amateurs here and there is fine, but sometimes it seems as if all the old county families have fled for Wisconsin, and we're being taken over by the green and in-the-dark. Just last week, a couple called me up and said their calves were all going batty – rolling their tongues, eating each other's tails, mooing all night. Ruth, this family had the calves in a stable together for a year. They plucked them away from their mothers, plopped them in front of a nursing machine, and fed them. As you can imagine, the calves were fat, and suckling on anything they could get their gummy mouths on. "The tongue rolling and hair eating is a stress response," I told them. "You have to let them out of the stable, let them see their mothers and nurse. Now what you have is borderline obsessive-compulsive cattle. They will be unstable cows until you get them straightened out, and that might never happen now." The couple held each other's hands and told me they invested twenty thousand dollars in these cows, pleaded with me to do something to fix the situation. I told them they should call a cattle consultant (yes, they exist now: so many changes), since my line of employment is merely tending to the body of the cattle.

If this is a new era, I want the old.

Love,
Foster

Dear Ruth,

I am concerned about Penny. Since you left, she seems to spend more and more of her waking hours in solitude and self-imposed confinement. She will return from work, mumble something inaudible, and shuffle to her room in silence. I am not sure if she is still depressed, or if she is simply unhappy at work. When I attempt to make conversation with her, to draw her out of her sullenness, she shakes her head and fixes herself a quick dinner. I don't think we have eaten a meal together since April. In the morning she inhales a bagel or a Pop-Tart and coffee, and for dinner she makes herself a fried egg sandwich or macaroni and cheese. Scurvy will be next in line if this continues. You are missed all around.

Doctor Coston tells me he doesn't know why I can't slumber. I told him I haven't slept more than two hours a night for weeks. His prognosis: stress, diet, chemical imbalance, or some combination thereof. In a medical journal last week I read about a new strain of fatal insomnia where the sufferer begins twitching and slurring speech, until experiencing random hallucinations and delusions, and finally death. I asked Coston about this, but he had no knowledge of it. He knows nothing of my other affliction, and I won't tell him

Nightly I drive to the Browns' farm and watch them chew and weave through the hills. I suppose it has become a sort of obsession. Recently, I have taken a flashlight, and surrounded by my bovine comfort, I read about famous recluses. This week I read about the desert hermits. I am flabbergasted by their self-chosen exile. I wonder if hermits ever ran from disgrace, and if so, what their disgraces may have been.

Tomorrow, I must give a calf a colostrum, remove the supernumerary teats. The Solteros tell me they can do the birth itself, but that they want me to do have the honor of the rest. This seems to be a gesture of pity. I told them about my financial state. They know I can't afford the doctors, much less my own practice. They think I am sabotaging my own profession, and perhaps I am. I can coast for a while and simply enjoy what I have.

Love,
Foster

Dear Ruth,

Today I had to attend to a lame cow, and unfortunately help Victor and Henry sedate several aggressive hounds. My existence seems to go in circles, never progressing. I must now assist within my own practice. What has become of my pride?

This was a salvageable day, however, since the Solteros called me to perform a Blockley test. Are they single-handedly trying to save my practice? I told them to feed the bull molasses – always good for a poor libido – however, they said they wanted the full run. The stanchioned cows were sedated to avoid the post-trauma, and after half an hour, they seemed even aroused by the scent of the bull. As two of the farmhands led the bull behind the first cow, I asked Jorge Soltero how many mounts he has noted over the past month, and he said none at all. "It seems he's shooting blanks," he said.

"Not that you can blame him with these dick teases around."

Watching a bull mate has become a feast for me. Not only the enormity of his genitalia, but the swift grace with which the bull copulates – all of it is tremendously arousing. The cow mooed, the penned sheep baaed, the chickens clucked, and the bull ejaculated into the cow. Calculated rape has a central role in animal husbandry, and it never ceases to disappoint. Mr. Soltero seemed pleased, and I was more than pleased. I admit my mindset might not be attractive to you, and I apologize. I am sorry. I am sorry.

I am sitting in my regular spot now, eating a cheese steak sandwich I purchased at Gregor's. Most of the cows are sleeping now. A cluster chomps on the tall weeds near the far oak tree. I wonder if Penny is sleeping, and if she dreams, and if she dreams, what she dreams. Does Penny ever write you? Though this is highly doubtful, I hope so for your sake.

Love,
Foster

Dear Ruth,

I am sitting in the sweltering house. I have decided not to use the air conditioner anymore. If the desert hermits didn't need to bathe or change clothes, I think I can do without air-conditioning. Penny hasn't said a word yet. Maybe she has been thinking the same thing. She spends even more time alone; she has all but stopped eating dinner, or at least as far as I can tell. I tried to ask her why, but she put her hands over her ears. I wonder when we will talk again. If she is that unhappy, why hasn't she departed? I don't want her to leave though. I feel closer to her, now more than any time since you left.

The Solteros called me back this morning. They said one fourth of their herd has heel flies, and they want me to come by and treat them. When I got there, I asked Mr. Soltero why he is being so kind to me – giving me business. He said he really wasn't trying to be nice, but that they have been neglectful (though it doesn't appear so to me) and had to pay attention to the health of the cows, since the milk has tasted rather acerbic. I simply think they are perfectionists.

They already had the sick cows penned for me, so it was easy. They overstated the case – maybe five cows had a mild case of heel flies, a few cysts, and hypodermal rash. I just used fenthion and phosmet and it was cleared up, though I squeezed out some of the flies in the cysts with my fingers so I didn't have to put these claves on the shelf any longer than they had to be. The Solteros had no idea heel flies wouldn't allow the cows to give edible milk. I told them they were lucky, and related the Brutherford situation a few years ago: over twenty paralyzed calves, seven of which died drooling, bloated, and riddled with dysphagia.

I have decided that tonight I will test the Browns' cattle. I'll let you know.

Love,
Foster

Dear Ruth,

It turns out that, no, cows cannot attain human venereal diseases (not that they don't have their own). I'm not sure if it goes the other way. I fell asleep on the Browns' hill last night, luckily waking at four before her help made its way down to the barn.

I was fortunate enough to be able to direct a birthing today. I have to confess it was quite erotic. I almost forgot what I was doing there, for I was so transfixed on the swinging udders. Seeing that thin tube of a calf slide out of Wilma made me ache for the Browns' hill. I am sorry to relate this to you, but I must remain exact with myself above all else.

However, I had to attend to a bull with wire worm and a large stomach worm. As you know, normally I prefer the energetic bull to the passive, ignorant cow, however, on this occasion, it was not the case. This was one ailing bull. Anorexia. Diarrhea. Edema. Hypoproteinemia. The poor bull was covered by lesions and could barely stand. I treated it the best I could, but I wonder if it might not be too late for him.

Tonight I didn't go the Browns. I was horrified by my own intentions. I suppose I do still retain a sliver of my old self. I stayed in my room, as Penny does. I didn't hear a peep emanate from her.

Love,
Foster

Dear Ruth

I am so sorry for everything I have done. I suppose I am a terrible person. All those wanderings, all those... Then the worst of it – what resulted in your body (never mind what it did to me). I don't blame you one bit for what you did. If animals had the means, I imagine many would also execute their rights in the way you chose. I don't think it was an easy out, rather a logical escape from pain. It's only natural.

I just petted the cows and milked them in the field. I will drink their milk from the source. At this point, who cares? As I squeezed their massive teats in my fingers, I couldn't help wish that women themselves were so ripe and helpless. The human world is too messy, overly complicated. If you'll forgive my offense, cows never complain as their human counterpart do daily. I can't go back now: I suckled directly from them.

Penny hasn't come home for three days. I have no idea where she is, or what she is doing. There is no sign of her. I hope she found peace, wherever she went. I spooked her several days ago. I was eating a hamburger at nine in the morning. She didn't understand this, although I tried to explain. "I feel close to the cows somehow," I told her. "I can't explain it. Their nature seems more to my liking." She just kept cussing, but not at me – in general. I haven't seen her since. I'm so sorry for everything.

Love,
Foster

Dear Ruth,

And I am sorry for being a misogynist pig, though you know I never meant any harm. Intention is the least of my problems: I'm selfish and greedy, and unable to control myself. Straight Fs for me. I shared a certain amount of intensity with people – you included. Maybe it wasn't love or tenderness, but it was something.

Tonight I brought the stool from home. The milk may have caused God knows what, but this is a minor concern at this point. I found a particularly friendly one who, I think, has been eyeing me. I roped her to the oak tree at the bottom of the incline, set the stool behind her. It was so gentle with that striking animal. She didn't fight me at all. Then I found another beauty, and she was just as sweet and considerate as the first. Oh, I have much potential here.

As usual, I left before four, and I blew sweet kisses to my entire lovely harem. Still, the stars seemed cold and remote. I was all alone.

Love,
Foster.

*

Printed in the United States
922000001B